ORON AMULAR

BOOK II: RITE OF PASSAGE

MICHAEL J HARVEY

malcolm down

PUBLISHING

23 22 21 20   7 6 5 4 3 2 1

First published 2020 by Malcolm Down Publishing Ltd.
www.malcolmdown.co.uk

British Library Cataloguing in Publication Data
A catalogue record for this book is available from the British Library.

ISBN 978-1-912863-38-9

Original cover concept by Arthur Dukes
Cover design by Esther Kotecha
Art direction by Sarah Grace

Printed in the UK

Oron Amular: Rite of Passage
is dedicated to my Soleithébar.
You enchant me more than you will ever know.

ACKNOWLEDGEMENTS

The love and support of many people has helped to bring *Oron Amular* into being. I owe a great debt of gratitude to those whose belief and encouragement sustained me in both the writing and the hunt for publication. I wish to thank my parents, Ian and Lucie, for raising me in a home of love and faith, and for setting my feet on this path. I reserve special thanks for Kelly Jamieson, for being so vocal a fan, right from the start, and for your friendship since. Phil Dobbs, it wasn't quite your thing, but you always encouraged me along the way, and never stopping asking about it. Pat Eisner and Matt Taylor also deserve my appreciation, for being among the first to read it, and for much practical support and helpful input. No one has done more to make this novel possible than my beloved wife, Lucy, my *Soleithébar*. Thank you for letting me have all those hours; thank you for believing in me; thank you for walking this road with me as the best of companions. Most of all, though, I wish to thank God, from whom comes every good and perfect gift (James 1:17). You gave me this imagination, these ideas, and this talent, and I honour You with every word written.

CONTENTS

SUMMARY OF BOOK I

In *The Call of the Mountain*, Book I of the *Oron Amular* trilogy, our adventure begins. Seeming chance has brought together the King of Maristonia and a mysterious wayfarer. In the city of Mariston they join forces to answer the summons of Kulothiel, the Mage-Lord, to a Tournament at the forgotten Mountain of Oron Amular. Lords, knights and champions from many lands have been invited to compete at this ancestral home of High Magic. The prize on offer, 'Power Unimaginable', is proving irresistible to all those thirsting for adventure and power. King Curillian is no different, though his motives might be nobler than some. Yet for all his strength and reputation, he does not know how to find the Mountain. The wandering conjuror Roujeark offers his services as a guide, for he has his business of his own at Oron Amular and has received a summons of a different kind. Together they set out, and braving many dangers by road and sea they embark upon the quest of Oron Amular. Yet they have not gone far before troubling news disrupts their plans. Circumstances force Curillian to take new counsel among the wood-elves who live on his borders. Beneath the eaves of the ancient forest of Tol Ankil he hears confirmation of the news that has troubled him. Despite the misgivings of Lancoir, his Captain of Guards, he pledges to rescue the elf princess Carea who has fallen into the hands of the evil mountain-dwelling harracks. His quest is no longer quite so simple, but is there also opportunity to be found in this dangerous diversion?

Map of
Astrom

© Michael J Harvey

Map of

**Oron
Amular**

Dorzand

Therenmar

Oron
Amular

Paeyeir

Black
Mountains

Kalimar

Marinia

Aranar

Arnorman

Faudunum

Stonad

Marindel

Dorzandwall

River Vanri

Firnon

Tol
Ankil

White
Hills

The
Bowl

Nimrell
Bay

Arkania
Forest

Aldia

The Armil Road

Markest

Arket

East Fold

Carthaki Mountains

The Saneth

Arten

Maristonia

Broadsword Ridge

Central Lands

River Ebrinon

Ebion

Delarom

Welton

Phirmar

Swordhilt Peninsula

Mariston

Carthaki Mountains

Pass

Sanbury

Laiston

Dagger's Cove

Mariston
Bay

© Michael J Harvey

I

Rock and Snow

ONCE Back at the bottom of the great tree, Curillian took Lancoir and Roujeark aside before they rejoined their companions and spoke to them. The journey back down the wooden walkway had been fraught with tension and unspoken disagreement.

'I know you are not in favour of this mission, Lancoir, but I will undertake it nonetheless. I ask no armist to come with me, and no pressed armist – you least of all – will I suffer in my company. Whoever comes, we must be few. We cannot carry war into the mountains with any hope. We will neither overmaster the harracks nor lay waste their cold citadel. Rather, it is as shadows and thieves we must go. With stealth we will penetrate their stronghold and steal the captive back. Therefore, there is no risk of the casualties you fear. But make your decision swiftly: either stay here with the main cohort, or come with my volunteers.'

Curillian went straight to bed then, letting no task come between him and sleep. Lancoir instead went and reviewed his kit. Roujeark went with him, seeing him as the more likely source of answers. They joined the rest of the King's Cohort in the lodge that had been made available to them. It was a wooden structure built into a bank of earth, so discrete that you hardly noticed it until you were right outside. A carved wooden doorway gave onto a wide hallway running back into the earth. The hall was filled with a long wooden table at which the

Royal Guards reclined in shirtsleeves. In their king's absence all had evidently been washed and well-fed, judging by the aromatic steam filling the air and the well-scraped bowls littering the table. Arms and armour had been piled to one side, and some of the guard had already taken to their beds in curtained niches cut into the walls. Overhead, the ceiling was a mass of tree-roots which had somehow been twined into wonderful patterns.

The happy banter died away almost immediately as Lancoir stomped in. Fists clenched, he took in the scene with a scowl and the armists' jests died on their lips. They knew the Captain of the Guard well enough to know when he was angry. Lancoir looked as if he might speak, and the armists braced themselves, but then he stalked off down the hall. Gradually the conversations resumed once he was past, and Roujeark felt the atmosphere recover as he followed the angry captain. Lancoir went right to the far end and sought out his own gear. Roujeark watched as the captain's anger seeped out in kit slammed down, weapons slotted resoundingly into scabbards and knots tied unnecessarily tight, the rope positively whistling and cracking in his hands. Some of the guards nearby were already asleep, but one or two were wakened and made nervous by their captain's ire.

'What are harracks?' Roujeark ventured to ask at last. Lancoir continued sorting his gear, but eventually answered.

'Harracks…' he snapped, but too loud, startling several others. He fixed each with a furious glare that made them turn away and mentally block up their ears. 'Harracks,' he repeated more softly, but hardly with less venom, 'are squat little bastards who live in the mountains that spawned them. They're so at home in stone that they're practically made of the stuff. Some say they're born of the stone itself. They're tougher than dwarves, slow-moving but ridiculously hard to kill. They blunt blades and smash shields. It's like trying to fight the mountains themselves. You've probably never heard of them, because the only time they've ventured down into the lowlands they've exposed weaknesses and been beaten, but get them in the mountains, around plenty of rock, and they thrive on it like elves in trees. That's why we've never taken them on at home, nor tried to flush them out, and that's why we shouldn't be trying now.' He thumped his backpack in frustration. Roujeark could tell that eavesdropping was still going on by the way some of the prone guards nearby jumped slightly in their feigned sleep.

Lancoir gripped his bag like he was going to rip the leather apart with his bare hands, but then slowly he relaxed.

'I just don't understand why he's doing it,' he said quietly, almost to himself. He was quiet for a moment. His next words were dropped so low that Roujeark had to lean in to pick them out. 'I've seen him impulsive before, we all know his quick-fire instincts on what's right, but never have I seen him risk so much for so little reason.'

Roujeark tried to mollify his wound-up companion. 'You heard the queen, Lancoir; all the great men of the world are on the move, converging for this tournament. Do you really want to miss out on that, or not even find out what's at stake?'

The captain was silent for a long time, eyes boring holes into his pack.

'No,' he conceded, muttering at the ground. 'We should be there.' Then suddenly he reached out and seized Roujeark's tunic and growled like a bear. 'But mark my words, Roujeark, nothing this big happens without trouble. The greater the prize, the greater the price.'

A

Shaken, Roujeark sat on his bed watching as Lancoir rooted out some volunteers. All thought of sleep was soon forgotten.

'Right, you deceitful dogs, I know you've been listening in. I know you're not asleep, so hear me now. Next bit of the mission's for a few only: I want a dozen volunteers to accompany myself and the king up into the mountains. Rescue mission. You know what's up there, so declare yourselves quick.' Roujeark felt dread creep up on him as he watched these courageous warriors daunted by this prospect. What's up there, he wondered, that they're so afraid of? Should I be more afraid? Piron and Surumo cast their bedding aside and stood up, but Lancoir instantly snarled them down.

'Not you Piron, you're not fit. Nor you, Surumo, someone's got to keep this rabble in order till we get back.'

The rest of the guards found it far harder to find their feet. Slowly, two stood up. A few moments passed and then another two stood also, and finally two more. Eventually twelve were standing. None could conceal their fear, but none were willing to back down now. Roujeark was both encouraged and dismayed to see his friend Andil among the standers.

'Andil, Aleinus, Haroth,' Lancoir called their names. 'Cyron, Edrist, Norscinde, Utarion, Antaya, Findor, Manrion. Good armists.' He paced up and down before them.

He surveyed the others, letting his gaze settle on two who were not Royal Guards. They were from the ragtag group that joined them at the royal hunting lodge. They wore different garb and had been sitting apart in a small group, yet nevertheless two of them now stood with the others.

'State your names.' Lancoir barked.

'Caréysin, sir,' said the one who was tall and slight.

'Lionenn,' said the other, not bothering to add 'sir'. He was shorter by far, but sturdier and thickly muscled. With a thick beard and mysterious marks upon his face, he was a fearsome sight to behold.

Roujeark noticed a great battleaxe resting just beside him. He looked a match even for Sir Lancoir. The captain was sizing them both up.

'Lionenn, Konenaire are you?'

'Aye.'

'Been in the mountains before?'

'Once or twice.'

'Good. Keep your axe sharp.'

'Ah always do.'

Lancoir turned on the other figure. 'And you? Do you have the profession to match your name?'

'Yes sir, never missed yet.'

'Good, don't start now.'

Lancoir moved away, and Surumo spoke. 'I'll await the king's orders for the rest of the cohort.'

Lancoir nodded.

'What of the other trackers?' Surumo asked, jerking his head in the direction of a surly group further up the hall.

'We'll think of a use for them,' said Lancoir, scowling at the group. 'They know their stuff in the mountains, and more of us may yet need to cross them. Await your orders. Stay alert.' He turned back to his kit, then suddenly whirled around and barked a name. 'Aleinus,' he singled out the armist who had been the first to stand. 'Aleinus, why are you going?'

The guard in question, who looked quite young, forced a smile of bravado.

'Captain, if the king is going to fall, how glorious will be the deaths of those who fall beside Curillian, greatest of the Harolins?' Lancoir growled acceptance of that.

'Glory in death is what we all seek,' said Haroth, morbidly.

Lancoir smiled grimly.

'As so you should. But make no mistake about it: you may not know what the game is yet, but Curillian won't fall before it's all played out. The only question is how many of us will die along the way.'

᛭

Curillian allowed them a day's rest. The following day, he woke before the dawn and walked through the mists. He didn't know who his volunteers were yet, but he knew they would be ready when he was. He had one last conversation to have before he left, so he followed the shadow through the misty trees. Leaving the leafy citadel behind he pursued the blackbird ahead of him, certain that it meant him to follow her. The bird left him some way behind, and he lost sight of it in the mists. Hurrying forward, he came to the mossy shore of one of the many lakes which dotted this northern part of the forest. There, standing on a great boulder in the shallows, the black-cloaked Dácariel stood, motionless. He joined her, walking through the water until he reached a small boulder beside the one she was standing on. She spoke practically at first.

'The easiest part of your journey is over.'

Easy? thought Curillian. I've had a ship burnt out from under me, been ambushed twice in my own realm, and many of my armists already lie dead. What does difficult look like? He voiced none of these thoughts, knowing she guessed them all too nearly.

'This seizure of Carea is not an isolated act,' she went on. 'The harracks have been very active of late, and my folk have seen them consorting with the goblins. They have given the snow-elves much trouble and even raided some of the high valleys of Kalimar itself. Together they are a great threat, and they may even attempt an invasion of the lowlands. My heart forebodes about the timing of their unrest, so close to the tournament…If you have forces nearby, it would be well to deploy them closer to the mountains, and have them closer at hand in the event of need…'

'I will do so, Lady. Those in my cohort not coming on the mission will redeploy to the foothills north of your realm, ready in case of trouble. They shall not impose on you any longer than necessary. By your leave, I have prepared orders for other units to march and join them. Indulge me and spare a guide to lead two of my messengers by the swiftest routes to the southern border – that way, word will reach my nearest legion as fast as possible. If you are in need, the Eastern Army of Maristonia will be on hand to assist you. Consider it a token of my gratitude for your hospitality.'

'It shall be done.' They fell silent for a while, and the mists enveloped them. When Dácariel spoke again, it was no longer about strategy.

'You're going to a lot of trouble, Curillian, to rescue her…' The queen left the thought hanging, neither wholly statement nor question.

'Lady, you know that I would go to her aid even if nothing else were at stake.' His voice was solemn, even though it was muffled by the mist. She turned imperceptibly towards him.

'They say that no armist and wood-elf have ever been joined in love. Yet I doubt that anyone has ever come closer than you and she.' Curillian was suddenly aware of her making intense eye-contact. 'Some thought the rumours grotesque. For myself, it only showed just how special you were, that you were able to move such a one as she in her soul. We all knew you were special, Curillian, right from when you were born. The Silver Emperor, the High King, myself, we all knew. And yet, it may be that your great deed in the judgement of history was to reclaim the throne of your forefathers after being exiled for so long; or that your greatest deeds came and went in the wars long ago. Think you that you can surpass the glory of your youth? So, I ask myself, what do you seek at this tournament? Power Unimaginable? You have already wielded great power, O King of Mariston. Glory has its limits. What makes you think that this great thing is not reserved for another?'

'There is only way to find out, Lady. I go to compete not merely for the prize, but to discover, if it may be, what Prélan's will is in all of this. My heart forebodes that this is merely the start of great and terrible things. I go also to strive for the best of myself. It has ever been so. I challenge the greatest, defy the deadliest, and strive to emulate the best and noblest. The quest for excellence has defined me.'

'No, Curillian, it has not defined you. There is no doubt that you will leave a mark on history of surpassing excellence and nobility, but those things do not define you. They are merely the symptoms of true greatness. You are, and always have been, defined by your love of Prélan, by the closeness of your relationship with Him. Verily, Prélan blesses abundantly those who walk with Him. What could you ever have achieved without His guiding, enabling Spirit? You may go and compete, O mortal king, but you must be ready, if, in this case, the will of Prélan differs from the desire of your heart. I do not ask much of you – just do as you always have done, walk with Him. You will not fall from greatness unless you fall from Him.'

He said nothing. Staring out over the water he contemplated her words. He did not look at her when he felt her long hand caress his cheek. The hand withdrew. He heard the flutter of wings and knew that she had changed and left him.

A

Lancoir, Roujeark and the twelve volunteers were ready. They stood outside the lodge with their gear, and to it their wood-elf hosts had added many valuable supplies.

'Nourishing food, and warm cloaks, to help keep you alive in the mountains,' one of the elves had said. The rest of the cohort had been reunited with their horses and expected to be going again soon, but word had got round about a chosen few being taken on a special mission, and now they were disconcerted. Through the mists Roujeark could make out their worried faces. With the king still gone, none of them knew what to do next, but they did not have to wait long. Curillian came back to them, solemn and quiet. He spoke first to the officers, Surumo and Piron, calling them forward.

'My friends, with great patience you have been kept in the dark till now and asked no questions. But no longer. Up to this point, all I've told you is that we are bound for an unusual gathering in Kalimar. I can now tell you: we are bound for Oron Amular, the Mountain of High Magic.' He gave a few moments for the words to sink in and the amazement to lodge in their faces. 'Yes, Kulothiel, Keeper of the Mountain and Head of the League of Wizardry, is hosting a tournament to which all the princes and champions of Astrom have been invited. Between us, we will contest momentous prizes. Roujeark, our new friend, is bound thither, and he will be my guide. But to persuade the elven High King to grant us passage, there is a task I must perform first. That is why I venture into Stonad, the land of the harracks, now. It is a rite of passage. When I return, successful, then the main quest can resume.'

'However, I do not ask you to sit here idle in a foreign place. New counsel has reached me, warning me of dangers close by and far off. The two swiftest riders, with wood-elf guides, must make haste to the southern border of the forest whence we entered and speed messages to General Horuistan of the 15th. He is to march the entire legion north and encamp between the north-western reaches of Tol Ankil and the River Amretu. You will attach the cohort to his force and be under his command, unless new orders reach you from me. Be alert, for you may well be called for before all this is over. While the messengers travel, the rest of you may take a few days' respite, but after that you must rendezvous with the legion. On no account should any of you return into the forest, and the main legion not at all. Is that understood?'

'I have my orders, sire,' said Surumo in acknowledgement. 'For my part, I am content. I have no desire to intrude into old legends. But our swords will be sharp and ready if you need us.' They both saluted, but Piron could not hide the longing in his face.

'I would go with you, sire,' he said plaintively. Curillian clasped a hand to his shoulder, then his neck.

'I know, Piron. But you're not yet fully fit, and you need to be for this mission. Gather your strength now, for there is plenty ahead of you, great deeds and danger alike.'

Roujeark watched the king brief his two officers, watched him answer their questions, and watched him bid farewell to his cohort of guards, who were desperately sorry to be parted from him. Not many were eager to march into harrack territory, but they had come to an alien place, and were uneasy about lingering here without their king. But such was Curillian's authority that they accepted his strange decision.

Then Roujeark noticed Queen Dácariel materialising as if out of the mist itself. Swathed in her tall black cloak, and accompanied by one of her formidable offspring, she watched the farewells before gliding to Curillian's side. She spoke soft words to him that only he could hear. He looked at the queen's companion and nodded.

'Lancoir, we are ready?'

The captain gave the barest inclination of his head, his face set grim.

'Good, then let us lose no time. Sin-Serin here will accompany us, and be our guide, as her brother was before. We march to the northern border of the forest, and thence into Stonad in the mountains beyond.' The armists all bowed their heads and each in turn received the elf-queen's blessing. Then she spoke words over them together.

'...*Tûh Prélan ábécos érese livon ey allédos rol amaluph*...May Prélan smile upon your mission and grant it success.'

⋀

Sin-Serin led them along a faded and ancient path through the trees. When dawn came, it drove away the gloom and revealed a fresh and glistening forest. Droplets of water left over from soft rain in the night dripped all around. They caught the sunlight as they did so and flashed, making the leaves look as if they were made of gold. The springy grass swayed in a light breeze and vestigial shreds of mist flitted amongst the trees.

The way was long on foot, and the ground was steadily rising, but Sin-Serin marched them at a stern pace and in four days they had reached the edge of the forest. They took their leave of the sentinels at the border and found that their feet were on an ancient and faded track. As they exited from under the eaves of the forest, they saw it march uphill, away north alongside the River Pharaphir, the parent river of the Sachill.

'Ought we follow the river?' Curillian asked of Sin-Serin. 'It will surely be watched.'

The elf nodded sagely. 'There is nothing for it. It is too easy to get lost in the mountains using any other path.'

So they climbed, nervous and watchful. At first the gradient was gentle, and the river lay open beside them under the sun, glinting in the warm light. It was not as hot as Roujeark was expecting out in the open air, but he did not realise how high they had already climbed – almost the same elevation as his home in the Tribune Valley, where the fierce heat of Maristonian summers softened into alpine warmth. He enjoyed the sun but, looking up, he saw that the foothills above them were beset by glowering clouds. He shivered looking at them. Gone were the days when the uplands had positive associations for him, happy childhood memories buried beneath a layer of pain.

On the first day, their path wound in zigzags up green slopes made damp by a hundred tiny rivulets racing to join the great river below. Roujeark was a little out of practice, but he was enjoying the hike. It was obvious, though, that the guards around him, less used to trekking in the uplands, were not so happy. On the second day, the grass gradually thinned out and lost its glossy green as browner hues started to take over. Where before they had marched through miniature forests of fern, now they trudged past clumps of heather, mossy hummocks and grass-crowned stones. Down below, the unobtrusive valley sides started to close in above the river and it shrank as it flowed past steepening slopes and overhanging banks. Behind them, the forest which had seemed so vast now looked small and far off. Looking down, Roujeark felt like he stood on the ankle of a giant whose legs the trees were forbidden to touch, such was the abrupt change between forest and hillside. Again he looked up, and the crags above him flitted in and out of dark clouds like furtive titans. With increasing regularity, the sun disappeared behind

24

clouds and swathes of shadow fell on the valley sides. The low clouds started to envelop them in an uncertain welcome. Time and again they paused to look back, but the receding forest was now only intermittently visible, peeking sometimes from behind curtains of wandering vapour.

Sin-Serin permitted them only rare and short breaks. Each time Roujeark paused, flushed with the effort of climbing, he soon became chilled and found himself piling on more clothing. Before long they were walking exclusively in clouds, condemned to dank, muted conditions. The temperature dropped alarmingly as a cold wind blew down from the mountains. It was a good thing that the king's foresight had made them well-prepared for an environment such as this. Warm layers were donned and over the top they had sheepskin coats and waxed cloaks to resist the moisture in the air.

'I'm rarely pleased to see clouds,' Roujeark overheard the king saying to Lancoir, 'but these are more than welcome – they'll hide us from unfriendly eyes.'

'For the moment...' came the guarded response.

They passed sidestreams braided with stones and caught occasional glimpses of the rocky staircases by which they had fallen into the main valley. They crossed more and more stretches of scree and loose rocks, which lay in their path like gnarled blankets casually draped across the hillsides. Ankles were turned and knees and shins were scraped. By the end of the second day, the landscape changed again. The tight valley suddenly opened up into a great U-shaped trough, flat-bottomed but walled with towering slopes fearsomely sheer.

The path, such as it was, led them past a spitting waterfall, which fell, as if from nowhere, out of an unguessed shelf above. Soon it was not just splashing falls which assaulted them with water: the damp mists in the air turned into driving rain and soaked them through. They made a sodden camp in the shelter of a low overhang of rock and conjured as good a meal as they could. The night was passed fireless and cheerless.

The morning, though, was splendid. Gone were the rains and the low clouds, and now revealed to their sight was a stunning theatre of rock. Roujeark had seen such places before, in the Carthaki Mountains. The more pious mountain-dwellers said that Prélan had scooped out the broad channels to display His majesty; the less pious were of the belief that they had been dug by giants to ease their travels. The wide valley looked like the empty hull of a rockship, and it stretched off into the mountains as far as they could see. Shimmering waterfalls cascaded down its flanks, gracing the sombre, rounded peaks above. Up at the rims of the valley, though, clouds lurked like distant spectators.

'Long ago,' Roujeark heard the king's voice beside him, 'when it pleased Prélan to keep the world colder, vast floods of ice gouged out these mountainous valleys like frozen warships, their broad prows snapping off all the rock that lay in their paths. In those times the world was changed, and what was once jagged became smooth.'

Roujeark listened with interest, hearing lore that was scarce heard by any outside the privileged class which could afford to attend Maristonia's universities.

'See the Pharaphir there, making its lonely way through the flat bottom of the valley? The river's all that remains of a monolith of ice – what the scholars call a glacier – which once would have soared so high as to fill this basin, right up to the rims.' Roujeark looked up at the cloudy rims, scarcely able to believe that all beneath had once been locked in ice.

'Somewhere up ahead,' the king told him as they trudged along together, 'way up in the mountains, where snow lies year-round, the Pharaphir probably still springs from a shrunken glacier, though I confess I've never seen it.'

'I've heard the tales of such places,' enthused Roujeark. 'Of high valleys where plains of ice groan like living things. And snow-folk dwell there, or so the story-tellers say...'

'Snow-folk?' Curillian laughed. 'I think they're a fairytale even to the elves.'

They would have continued to wander, marvelling, through that mighty open-air cavern, but Sin-Serin took them close to the cliff-like sides and had them hugging the steep slopes as they walked.

'This is the harracks' porch,' she said. 'Our knowledge stretches no further, but we know this is the beginning of their domain. We must take great care.'

From then on, they grew to dread every stone-fall and constantly craned their necks up, fearfully expecting hidden foes to reveal themselves in ambush. Rounding a bend in the valley, they saw that the valley did not stretch on unimpeded for ever, as it had at first seemed, but was filled with a great narrow ridge, tall and sharp as a ship's prow. Shard-like, and obsidian-dark, it virtually cut the great rounded trough into two smaller valleys. Two branches of the Paraphir opened out, rushing either side of the ridge.

A bitingly cold wind rushed down from the mountains to greet them, and they felt the temperature plummet. With the wind came fresh clouds and new rain, icy cold this time. Their discomfiture soon turned to concern as the rain started to harden into snow. They trudged onwards, sometimes leaning acutely to keep making progress against the wind. The vicious precipitation stung their faces and any other patch of flesh left exposed. None of their voices had been raised above murmurs for days now, but Curillian had to shout into Sin-Serin's ear just to be heard.

'Which side of this ridge ought we to go?' The wood-elf seemed unsure. She, too, shouted to make her response audible.

'I do not know – it is likely that any path up this valley will take us to the stone city.'

The king made his decision for her.

'We go left.'

Roujeark grew more and more miserable – the snow showed little sign of letting up, and if anything the air seemed to grow colder, making his throat and nostrils smart. His feet were well-shod, but even so he began to feel them grow damp. Curillian led them now, since Sin-Serin had come to the limit of her knowledge. Desperate to gain some shelter from the terrible wind, the king led them to the western side of the left-hand valley. There they were sheltered from the worst onslaught, and found a narrow path cutting up the rock-face. Barely broad enough to walk on, it seemed to have been purposefully created, but so many rocks, fallen from the heights above, littered the way that it was hard to be sure.

They forged up for as long as their strength held out, and then they were forced to stop. They made the most of a little overhang to shelter from the snow and minimise the risk of being struck by falling stones. They swept out the worst of the encroaching snow and laid out blankets. Their wet cloaks they took off and fastened to the overhang as crude windbreaks, replacing them with spare dry cloaks. Roujeark huddled down, shivering, and found himself between two different conversations. To his left, the king and the elf debated in low tones.

'This is a fierce storm for early *Pleuviel*, anyone would think we had set off in winter. The snow is already shin-deep on the track ahead, it must have been snowing here for some time,' the king surmised.

'Snowstorms can strike at any time in the mountains. It may shelter us from the harracks,' Sin-Serin replied. 'But it will be perilous as we climb higher. You may find that the weather is a worse enemy to you and your comrades than any stone-foot.'

On his right, several of the guards were grumbling, teeth chattering, as they huddled together and tried to keep warm.

'Coming up here was a fine idea, wasn't it? Hope our bloomin' guide knows where she's taking us.'

'Look at her there in her tunic and thin cloak, hardly affected by the cold. Maybe she doesn't feel it?'

'Or maybe she's too proud to show weakness in front of us...'

'She's magic, just like that elf-lady back in the forest. It'll be her magic keepin' her warm.'

'Well why doesn't she bloody well share the goods?'

As if to take herself away from their envious looks, Sin-Serin disappeared off into the snow, and Curillian ducked under the overhang to join them.

'Whatever magic she has, she isn't using it right now.' Apparently he had overheard, or guessed, their conversation. 'Elven powers are less potent up here in the mountains, just as the harracks are weaker when out of their element; any attempt to use unnatural abilities here would send an unmistakeable signal to watchers.'

Roujeark looked up at those words, but the idea vanished just as soon as it had appeared – he was too cold to think about any magic.

'Right now,' the king went on, 'she is simply scouting ahead. If she appears to be less susceptible to the cold than us, it is simply because of the natural grace bestowed on elven constitutions. It was the same with men once, long ago, before they turned away from Prélan and forfeited many of His blessings. Now, though, try to get some sleep, we'll move off before dawn.'

True to the king's word, Lancoir roused them all while it was still dark. The barest glimpse around their improvised curtains told them it was still snowing, and that it had accumulated deeply on the narrow path outside. They awoke deeply stiff and unspeakably cold. It took a lot of stamping and flexing before Roujeark could even feel his fingers and toes. They moved off carefully, practically wading through the snow, knowing that even a slight miscalculation could send them sliding down the sheer slope to their right. Sin-Serin was back with them, but if she had gleaned any particular insights on her reconnaissance, she did not share it with them.

Roujeark was no longer merely miserable, just deeply worried. A child of the mountains, he had never known exposure like this. His experiences of snow had been limited to brief forays, and during the heavy stuff he and his father had kept snug inside next to the fire. He was not sure how much longer he could last in conditions like these. Full springtime might be burgeoning down on the plains below, but up here in the mountains winter could re-exert itself whenever its capricious mood took it. Up ahead, he heard one of the guards complaining to Lancoir.

'Why don't we go back? We'll die in this snow without shelter or fire…' Lancoir, though, was unmoved.

'We will not go back. We will make use of this snow for as long as we can. Endure it or be left behind.' Whatever discomfort he himself was feeling, Lancoir, tougher than all of them, was ruthless in dragging the others along with him.

And so they plunged on, braving the snow as best they could. Several times they heard ominous rumblings above them and were soon after showered with snow falling down from the cliff. On one such occasion, Aleinus, the first volunteer, was nearly knocked off the path and into thin air, prevented only by the steady hand of Lancoir, who reached out and caught him.

After an interminable stretch of time, their path seemed to bring them above the level of the trough-valley's rim, for the ice-sheened rock wall on their left gave out. Shaking with cold, Roujeark was dimly aware of gentler slopes stretching away into a blurry distance. All was white here, covered in snow deeper than any they had yet come across. An ill-judged step brought the snow up to his waist, and he had to be tugged out by two of the guards. He could no longer feel the deadly burn in his limbs, and an eerie numbness started to settle over his body like a suffocating blanket. He lost all awareness of where the others were in relation to himself. He barely heard the latest rumble, although it was louder than the ones before. A deep thrumming built up in his ears, soon accompanied by waves of crunching, coming rapidly nearer. Too late he looked left and his vision was filled with a powdery juggernaut. His feet were swept out from under him, his mouth and nose filled with snow and he instantly lost sight of his companions. Terrified and panicking, he was carried along, now submerged in the snow, now just gasping clear. He was turned over and over and around until finally he came to a halt, thoroughly disorientated. By great luck, in his final position he was only covered by a thin film of snow. Scrabbling frantically at it he broke through and glimpsed the muffled grey of the world above. Fleeting relief was soon swamped by a lethargic blackness which stole over him. In the last few seconds before losing consciousness, he heard soft feet crunching near him, and then, as his eyelids slammed shut, a pale shadow reaching down to him.

II

In the Company of Legends

ROUJEARK Came to and did not know whether he was still in this world or in the next. Wherever he was, he was resting, and the space around him was warm. A pale blue light was about him. Feeling was coming back into his limbs and they burned like fire. His head swam. Gingerly exploring his environment with his fingers, he felt thick furs under him, soft and warm. Looking up, he could see nothing except a blue haze. Gradually though the details filtered through, and he felt sure his eyes were telling him that they could see a ceiling of ice – neatly shaped into blocks – but ice nonetheless. The incongruity of it baffled him. Where was he? He had no memory of coming here; he must have been brought. He turned his head one way, and saw a figure lying beside him. One of the guards, pale and unmoving. Caréysin, he thought. Yes, his bow lay beside him, unbroken. He turned his head the other way. On the other side of him was another figure, another guard, Lionenn, clasping his great axe.

It wasn't until he mustered the strength to sit up that he began to make sense of it all. He was in an enclosed space, barely a dozen feet wide. A low domed ceiling ran overhead. Whiter light peeped through cracks in the blocks to pierce the pervading bluish hue, and through a small aperture like a vent. Both the walls and the ceiling were made of ice. The only way of exit was a narrow tunnel opening out of the wall. Despite the cold light, it was oddly snug. Inside were his companions. Or most of them. Arrayed with their feet inward to form a snug circle, they were packed into the ice-chamber as tight as sardines in a pan. All were out cold, showing no signs of life, except two who were sitting up like him. Lancoir and Curillian both had their knees drawn up to their chests, and both looked drawn and pensive. Roujeark started to share their sobriety as his curiosity about his surroundings gave way to concern about his companions. Two of the guards and Sin-Serin were missing, even after he had recounted twice. He did not know them all by name yet, but three were definitely missing.

The king and the captain did not seem about to be forthcoming, so Roujeark resumed his inspection of their accommodation. Each armist had ample furs both under and over him, wrapping them in a cocoon of warmth, and the collective generation of body heat made for a very comfortable atmosphere. As the warmth and life flowed back into him, he became impatient.

'What is this place?' What he had thought was just a whisper seemed devastatingly loud in that confined place, and his own words rang in his ears. No one answered him. Perhaps even the all-knowing Curillian was as mystified as he. Then there came a scuffling from the tunnel, and all eyes turned that way apprehensively. It continued, growing louder, until an odd conveyance emerged from the tunnel's mouth. A long sled glided into the small space between two of the sleeping figures. Bulky-looking contents were well-wrapped in skin covers and ropes. Once it had nosed fully into the chamber, the person who had been pushing it entered in after it. Roujeark watched a lanky white fur-clad figure unfold itself and stand upright, pushing back its heavy hood as it did so. Underneath was a tall face, delicate yet gaunt, and covered with thick hair the colour of liquid silver. Yet Roujeark saw nothing but the eyes. Two piercing eyes of a blue so pure and deep they couldn't possibly be real. Twin pools of icy sapphire they were, beautiful, and utterly transfixing. They regarded each of the figures in turn, and if any expression could be read in them, it was neither hostility nor love, but curiosity. Curillian gaped back, with as much unabashed amazement as the other two.

'I thought you were a legend...' he breathed, barely loud enough for Roujeark to catch the words. Unoffended and uncomprehending, yet apparently satisfied by her silent survey, the newcomer bent over her sled, deftly threw back the wrappings and produced, as if from nowhere, bowls and spoons made of horn. Roujeark marvelled as he watched a pot uncovered. Its cunning fastening was removed, and steam sprang forth. All of a sudden, the small space was filled with a wonderful aroma. Roujeark's stomach growled volubly, but just as he had plucked up the courage to address the strange host, the newcomer left as suddenly as she had arrived, darting back into the tunnel with the litheness of a mountain-cat.

Roujeark and Lancoir looked at each other for a moment, and then they both lunged for the food, only Curillian maintaining his dignity. They scarce had time to admire the cunning of the pot's placement and portability, so absorbed were they by the food. It turned out to be a broth, full of strips of meat and fragrant with rock-herbs. The meat was of some lean mountain-creature, tough and stringy. It would have been considered uncouth at a genteel lowland banquet, but here, after near-death in the snow, it was satisfying beyond measure. Those guards who had not been roused by the heavenly aroma were soon awakened and given horn bowls full of the nourishing broth. They did not speak, and before they were finished eating, the stranger came back. This time she came with Sin-Serin in tow, the wood-elf looking quite at ease and none the worse for wear.

With ever so slightly more friendliness in her startling eyes than before, their mysterious host surveyed them once again and then spoke a few words in a soft, melodious language. It was as soft and furtive as snow, quite unlike the tongue spoken among the wood-elves, yet lovely in its own way. Sin-Serin interpreted for them, though even she did not seem wholly fluent.

'Aiiyoshaa of the Cuherai declares that you are welcome, and bids you follow her to her house.'

They were given no chance to respond, for even as the words finished leaving Sin-Serin's lips the mysterious Aiiyosha vanished again, diving into the tunnel. The wood-elf wordlessly ushered them to follow, and so, one by one, they entered the tunnel. Only when he tried to bend down did Roujeark realise just how stiff and weak he was. And there was small comfort to be had in the tunnel, which was cold and alarmingly narrow. The ice was painfully cold under hand, so he pulled down the sleeves of his coat to cover his palms. They had no idea where they were going, but from up ahead, the scuffling of their more agile host came echoing back to them. It was just as well, for they came to a junction in the tunnel, where two ways branched off at right angles to each other, and only the sound coming from ahead told them which to take.

The journey was not actually that far – it just seemed to drag on because their awkward limbs made heavy weather of it – and eventually they came to an opening. They stood upright in another warm blue chamber, but this one was larger than the one they had left. Furs and patchwork quilts hung from the icy walls, and deep recesses lined the far wall. More thick furs were spread lavishly on a raised circular area in the chamber's centre. There sat Aiiyosha, with two others beside her. All were cross-legged and dressed alike, and all regarded the king's party with the same intelligent ice-blue eyes. They were gestured to come and sit with the trio of fur-clad figures. As he settled himself stiffly down, Roujeark could scarcely see any differences between the three hosts, except two were female and one male. Aiiyosha, in the centre, spoke again, and Sin-Serin translated the same welcome as before.

'Aiiyosha of the Cuherai bids you all welcome, children of the southern mountains.'

Curillian bowed low, and then, once seated, introduced himself and his companions.

'Curillian, son of Mirkan, king of Maristonia am I, and these armists with me are members of my royal guard...'

Aiiyosha spoke again and watched Curillian as the translation was made.

'Here among the Cuherai we do not count ancestors or titles, for we are few, and we are simple.' More words were spoken, and Sin-Serin dropped the first person. 'She says she is the daughter of Cuherl, which makes her a princess among the snow-elves. She and her family are the only ones of their folk living in this part of the mountains, although others are elsewhere.'

Now Curillian had something to go on. Like everyone not of that race, he had believed the Cuherai, the snow-elves, were a myth, a unique people long since vanished from the world, if they had ever walked it, but the name of Cuherl was familiar, for the great lineages of the three elf-kindreds of Kalimar were still part of a Harolin prince's education. Cuherl was the great-grandson of Marintor, king of the sea-elves, and therefore his daughter Aiiyosha was in the equivalent generation of her kindred as Sin-Serin was in hers, separated from the head of the kindred by four generations. The wood-elf addressed their host directly in her own tongue.

'Let me say again, Aiiyosha, how honoured I am to come into your home. Alas, too seldom do the children of the wood and of the snow meet, but I am delighted to make your acquaintance.' Aiiyosha nodded in acknowledgement, and then spoke in Curillian's direction again.

'She says that two of your party were lost in the avalanche. They were buried too deeply by the snow, beyond reach. She says she is sorry.'

Curillian could see the sympathy and sorrow in his host's face and was amazed at how tangibly the feelings were etched there. Eons of dwelling in this rarified world of ice and snow had clearly done nothing to stem the expression of emotions.

After an appropriate pause, more words came. 'She wants to know why you have left your realm and come to hers,' Sin-Serin told Curillian.

Curillian told the brief tale of their mission in the mountains, how they had come from Tol Ankil with Dácariel's blessing to rescue Carea, whom they believed was being held captive by the harracks of Faudunum. At the mention of those last two names, the sympathy went out of Aiiyosha's face, and those of her companions, and all three made hostile growling noises.

'So, they're not any fonder of the stone-foots than we are...' muttered Lancoir to Roujeark, earning a brief, mercurial glance from Aiiyosha. The snow-elf chieftain regarded Curillian for a long time, and then spoke through Sin-Serin again.

'She says you are a friend of hers if you are not a friend of the harracks, but she hopes you will not bring about trouble for her people. The Cuherai avoid the harracks and the harracks avoid them, but a confrontation in the cold city might spell danger for her family. She wants to know what you plan to do.'

'Tell her we are very grateful for her succour, without which we would all be dead, and that the last thing we want is to repay her with distress. Yet we cannot leave our mission unfulfilled. I simply intend to rescue the princess, getting in and out as quickly as possible. I do not intend to confront the harracks or fight them any more than is necessary. She has done much for us, and we are in her debt, but can she help us further, in Prélan's name?'

Curillian held the snow-elf chieftain's eye as his plea was conveyed, and waited quietly as she weighed it up. The three snow-elves turned slightly towards one another and conversed in tones so soft that the armists would have been unaware of it had everything else not been so quiet. After a long discussion they turned back to their guests, and Aiiyosha spoke her answer.

'She says she will give you food and supplies to keep you on your way; what is more, she says she will lead you back to the path to Faudunum, for we are far out of the way here, and much higher up. Yet neither she nor any of her folk will go with you to the city or raise arms to help you.'

After the main message was delivered Aiiyosha spoke a final sentence, softer than the rest. Sin-Solar hesitated before passing it on. 'She says that if any of her people come to harm, you will none of you leave the mountains alive, though you may escape Faudunum.'

⋏

The armists returned to their own chamber, but Sin-Serin remained behind, closeted with her distant kin. They mourned their comrades who had fallen, praying for their souls and drinking a toast of the snow-elf cordial in their honour. Manrion and Haroth were their names, brave warriors now buried deep in the ice, far from home.

In spite of their weariness, Curillian pressed them to haste, adamant that they should leave soon, and that time was running short. So, they made sure they were ready to leave as soon as Sin-Serin returned. More snow-elves, who might have been Aiiyosha's sons and daughters, came and brought them packs of food and skins of a sweet and refreshing cordial. They also gave them fur garments which were much warmer than the clothes they had brought with them. The armists tried to convey their gratitude, but the snow-elves merely smiled and took their leave without speaking. Some time after they left, Sin-Serin returned, and Curillian was eager for further information from her.

'I have learnt much from Aiiyosha and her folk. It seems we took a wrong turn back in the valley,' the elf told him. 'We should have gone to the right of that great ridge, not left. But going right would have led us to the harracks' first outpost. Coming this way, though it has brought us trouble, perhaps spared us trouble of a worse sort. The Cuherai were aware of us before ever the snow fell. They kept a close eye on us, and so were at hand when the avalanche came. Those of us who could be saved were hauled from the snow and borne miles uphill to the abode of the Cuherai, where we now rest. Since today is already far gone, we will leave with first light on the morrow, and the Cuherai will guide us. We are far above the valley of Rumuron, a rocky brother of Pharaphir, but they will lead us back to that valley, only further along. They say we should not be worried, for the snow is not so bad across the river. Apparently, there is a rope-bridge above Rumuron's rapids. Once across that stream, and the dry gorge beyond, we will be in sight of a harrack fort and the track to Faudunum, and thus be able to guide ourselves.'

⋀

In the morning, they reluctantly left their shelter. This time taking the other route at the fork in the tunnel, they crawled up a slope and emerged out into the open. Roujeark gasped as a blast of chill wind hit him. The air was thin and cold, and he felt light-headed. Then his eyes took in the view, and he was amazed. From this glistening snowfield, a wide panorama of the mountains could be seen. Mountain peaks, hard and black and draped with ice, rose behind them, and before them the ground fell away into the valleys far below. They all stood and stared, awed by the majesty of the view. None of them had realised how high up they had come.

'Where there is snow, there the harrack treads not,' Aiiyosha told them through Sin-Solar. Then she produced strange shoes for them to wear. Wide and circular, they were made of light wooden frames criss-crossed by strings of animal tendon. They strapped them to their hob-nailed boots and suddenly found that they could walk on the snow without sinking. Now they could look at the snowfield differently – it was no longer a wearisome barrier to be crossed only with great difficulty. Thus-equipped, they made good progress downhill, led by the snow-elf chieftain, who was towing a heavily laden sled. At one point she stopped and called Sin-Solar and Curillian to him. Pointing away to the north-east, she uttered a single word.

'Faudunum.'

Curillian traced her finger down to the valley, which just showed as a slit in the ground. Then, he followed the valley along as far as it could be discerned. Although he could not see the city, he now knew roughly where it lay. For the meantime, though, they carried on downhill, barely pausing and hardly speaking all day. Only at the end of the first day did the snow start to thin out. Now it was no longer a deep field, but a thin blanket. Aiiyosha led them into a secret shelter, which had been completely invisible to them until she revealed it. It seemed to be some sort of frequently used outpost of the snow-elves, for inside were bedding, sleeping compartments, and best of all, stores of food. They ate heartily, then rested gratefully in that place, nursing aches in a whole different set of muscles after the long downhill march.

When they left in the morning, the entrance to the shelter vanished to sight as soon as Aiiyosha concealed it again. Though they took great precautions, Roujeark thought, the snow-elves really didn't need to worry about anyone finding their shelters. Halfway through that second day, still descending steeply, they came to the edge of the snowline, where the ground beneath starting patching through. Aiiyosha halted abruptly.

'She will go no further,' Sin-Serin told them. 'But fear not, she has told me the rest of the way.'

Now they saw what the sled was carrying. The snow-elf chieftain unloaded it of packs of food, one for each of them. They gratefully stowed them in their own packs and gave her thanks. Curillian bowed low and thanked her again. Aiiyosha seemed somewhat bemused by their manners, but she did not drag out the farewell. She placed her hands on Sin-Serin and Curillian in turn, and uttered over each a blessing in her own tongue. Then she was gone. At first, they watched her amazingly nimble progress back up the mountain, but very soon they lost her amid the snowy contours.

'Well,' said Lancoir, 'I doubt if we'll see her again.'

'Maybe not,' answered Sin-Serin, 'but she'll see us. They have eyes capable of following us wherever we go in these mountains. Do not take her threat lightly.' Then the wood-elf turned to Curillian and spoke softly to him as they surveyed the terrain below them.

'After you left on that first night, Aiiyosha told me a strange thing. She said that one of her kin has gone missing. Apparently, he vanished in the vicinity of Faudunum.'

Curillian looked up at her. 'What? Why would one of their kind stray so near the stronghold of their enemies?'

'It is strange indeed.'

'Well,' said Curillian, 'maybe we'll end up rescuing two captives, not one.'

'Perhaps,' the elf agreed. 'Or we may end up repaying our host in a different way.'

Curillian did not stop to ponder Sin-Serin's riddle, but struck off downhill, eager to be going. He was conscious of time ticking away – they only had until the first moon of summer to reach Oron Amular, and he still had no idea how long yet was the road thither.

After a few more hours of tramping they came back to the rim of the valley and found that it plummeted down no less sharply here than further down where they had left it. Its side was like a cliff dropping away beneath their feet. Looking out across it, they saw the same high ridge rising out of the valley floor, sheer and precipitous. They watched eagles launch themselves from eyries nestled in its impossibly steep sides to patrol the skies. Behind the knife-edge ridge the opposite rim could just be seen, with rugged slopes rising beyond. There would have been no way across but for the bridge. It was a rickety structure of ancient wood and rope, swaying and creaking in the breeze. None of the guards looked keen to use it.

Curillian and several others advanced up to it. Lancoir tested the first plank doubtfully with his foot and jerked the rope hand-rail. They all watched the whole bridge shudder and jump about like a skittish colt, and nerves fluttered in their bellies. For Roujeark, though, there was a deeper dread. Apprehension flooded him, making all his senses tingle and the hairs on the nape of his neck stand on end. He scanned both sides of the gorge with deep misgivings.

'Clearly this was not put here for our convenience,' said Curillian.

'This bridge can only have been put here by the harracks,' mused Sin-Serin, 'for the Cuherai would need it not.'

'And yet they cannot use it often,' observed the king. 'See what bad repair it is in. If they do not like to come near the edge of the snow-elves' territory, then perhaps there is hope that we may cross in peace.'

Sin-Serin gave answer enough by remaining silent, doubt etched in her normally unreadable face. Lancoir voiced his own thoughts.

'Consider, my king, were we to cross, this would be our only retreat from trouble. I like not the thought of such a bottleneck at my back.' He gave the bridge another speculative shove to emphasise his point. Curillian nodded, acknowledging the fact. He looked to Sin-Serin, who seemed absorbed in private concentration.

'Can you...change?' the king whispered to his elven guide. Disquiet furrowed the elf's smooth forehead.

'Would that I could,' she whispered softly. 'A hostile will pervades the valley and I find my senses diminished in this strange environment. The chances of successfully completing even a simple *morph* are slim, and even if I could, it would merely serve to announce our presence.' Roujeark had not heard the elf's words, but he, too, sensed animosity in the air, even if he couldn't say what caused it. Having weighed up what both Sin-Serin and Lancoir had said, Roujeark now saw the king turning last to him. In spite of his fear, he could not help but feel a stab of pride at being consulted along with such veterans.

'Roujeark,' Curillian said to him. 'You have been more attuned to danger than any of us on this journey – what do your instincts tell you?'

'It scarcely needs to be said that we are in danger, Lord, but I cannot tell from what quarter it will first assail us. All I know is that I feel sure our peril will increase with every step taken from now on.' Curillian went quiet, taking counsel last of all with himself. They watched him staring out across the chasm. He gripped the sides of the bridge with both arms, as if trying to gauge its reliability through touch alone. Finally, he swung around to look at them again.

'We will cross.'

Roujeark's heart jumped in alarm – he had felt sure the king would veer away and find another route. But no, he actually meant to attempt it. Curillian saw his doubt, and the same doubt in the others, and addressed it.

'Our quest lies on the other side of this gorge.' He pointed across the gulf. 'And I mean to fulfil it. And since I see no other way, we will tread this bridge.'

Even Lancoir's devotion faltered in that place.

'I implore you…Curillian…do not…'

'I will not turn back,' the king said sharply. His eyes glared out, challenging the fear in them. When he saw them hesitating still, he spoke again. 'I will cross, alone if needs be.' With that he set foot to the first plank and trusted his weight to it. With hardly a falter he took another step, and another. It took barely a heartbeat longer for the magnetism of his will to drag them after. Lancoir started after him, and then the other guards. Trembling, Roujeark joined them, and last of all came Sin-Serin, as calmly as if she had meant to bring up the rear all along. One split-second glance down at his feet, and the gaping emptiness beneath, convinced Roujeark not to look down again. Feeling sick and faint, he kept his eyes firmly on the guard in front of him. Gripping the sides fiercely with both arms tensed, he felt every vibration and wobble made by the others. The whole bridge seemed to lurch and bounce up and down like a living thing as they inched forward. His feet felt for the planks almost with a sense of their own. The planks were not as evenly spaced as he might have wished, and without the collaboration of his eyes he more than once stumbled into a gap or lost his footing. Each time his heart thundered and his head swam. There were stunning vistas to both sides, but they were completely lost on him. He would have closed his eyes altogether, but the gusting of the wind made him feel like he would be blown into oblivion if he did not keep them open.

When he felt they were roughly halfway across, he started to feel a bit more composed. But then he realised the guard in front of him had stopped. Obliged to stop himself, he felt the vibration of footfalls fading away until it was just the natural movement of the bridge he could feel. Why had they stopped? Another glance down, into the deepest recesses below, brought all his panic to the surface again. Looking sharply up again, he repositioned himself marginally to be able to look up ahead, leaning as far out as he dared. They were situated in the greatest extent of the bridge's sag, and from that precarious position they had to look up quite a way to see the top.

Someone was standing at the far end of the bridge. Short and stocky, a dark figure stood framed between the posts and the sky behind.

Roujeark looked round as quickly as his nauseated state would allow him, and all was clear behind them. They could still retreat. But the king advanced instead, treading up the steepening gradient with bold determination. Then he stopped again, and Roujeark saw why. More figures could now be seen, and still more, until they clustered around the bridge's exit in a forbidding obstacle.

'Back!'

Lancoir's shout, buffeted by the wind, barely reached him, but when Roujeark and the others looked behind again another figure, exactly the same as those in front, suddenly materialised to bar the entrance to the bridge. Both sides were sealed. They were trapped. Roujeark and those near him took several steps back, thinking one was better odds than many, but even as they did so more figures appeared as if from nowhere to reinforce the one. Through waves of nausea Roujeark tried to reach the mysterious power within him, but it wouldn't come. What before had emblazoned itself boldly if illegibly in his mind now fled before the groping fingers of his mind like shreds of smoke in a gale. He stretched out his hands, but nothing would come, and the instant loss of security made him seize the rope again quicker than thought. The newcomers made no sound, but they remained eerily and immovably in place. Above the wind's blasts, only the murmurs of fear of those near him could be heard. The elite soldiery of Maristonia had hitherto seemed fearless, but now they quailed. It was the only realisation at that point which could have disconcerted Roujeark further.

A tremor running through the wood and through the rope announced the intrusion of heavy feet onto the bridge. Still none of them knew what to do, and icy fear coursed through Roujeark's veins. He heard the scrape of swords being drawn, more in desperation than out of any realistic thought of success. Slowly, unstoppably, the grim figures thumped further onto the bridge from both sides. Roujeark steeled himself for the end. An arrow sprang from Sin-Serin's bow in front of him as the only defiance from the little party, but though it found its mark unerringly in the lead figure, it had no effect, and the figures kept coming. Resignedly, the elf put her bow away and drew her long daggers. Just then Roujeark felt an almighty tremor run through the bridge, more violent than anything yet. His hand leapt involuntarily away from the rope-side as if burned, and the whole bridge lurched. The structure beneath swayed drunkenly, as if being rocked by some new force, and when he turned around again to the front, he saw why. Curillian had hurried forward, as close to the advancing foes as he dared, and taken to the rope-side with his sword. Roujeark put his hand back to the rope only to feel the tension it in vanish like a whiplash. He staggered, somehow managing to keep his footing. One side of the bridge was cut. Now it sloped dangerously to one side.

'HOLD ON!'

The king's bellowed warning came back to them even as his first stroke landed on the other side. The keen metal shore straight through the top rope in one cut. Roujeark felt his bowels weaken and his legs give way as the loosened integrity of the bridge communicated itself through his feet and fingertips. Their accosters, having seen the danger and hurried to thwart it, were nearly on Curillian now, but with one last swing he severed the bridge. One moment the fading support of the bridge gave the illusion of safety beneath Roujeark, the next it fell away beneath him in an awful whoosh. The speed of his survival instincts, swifter by far than any reflex or intention, was all that saved him as he clutched unthinkingly at the disappearing rope strands. Another moment and the drag of gravity would have wrenched it beyond his grasp and left him to plunge freely into space. Having seized the rope with one hand, he swung himself round and grasped a plank with the other, holding them both tight with desperate strength. Hanging on for dear life, he was hurtled through empty space like a slingshot. The gut-wrenching heave that accompanied it felt like some capricious force was trying to inwardly rearrange his bodily organs. Now, facing inward, he could see the cliff-wall speeding towards them like the end of existence. He barely heard his own shrill scream, subtle as an extra keen edge to the wind.

He screwed his eyes tight shut and clenched his whole body ahead of the dreadful impact. Nothing could have prepared him for the bone-crunching, breath-depriving, thought-swamping, reality-shattering force of it. His feeble grip was loosened in an instant and he was falling, rock and wood and rope flashing upward past his terrified eyes in a kaleidoscope of incomprehensible motion. He tried to snatch at the bridge as it tore past, but his fingers could find no purchase. No sooner did they touch wood than it was wrenched away again. Almost imperceptibly his rate of fall decelerated, just enough for him to achieve a fleeting finger-hold. Once, twice, he managed to check his downward progress before losing his grip and falling again. Utterly aware of those falling above and below him, his world shrunk to just a narrow shaft of consciousness intent upon somehow living through this. At last his fingers caught again, and oblivious to the wrenching pain shooting from the nails through to his shoulders, he felt himself shudder to a stop. He had no idea of how far he had fallen or had left to fall; he just felt his battered body hanging by the frayed strand of his own strength.

He held on just long enough for the *what now?* thought to occur to him, and then he failed himself. He could hold on no longer. He lost his grip. Eyes struggling to focus dimly reported a length of rope flitting by as the last hope, but even as his hands successfully reached it the dangling length blistered through his palms, taking the skin with it. Then he was falling unchecked again. Something hard yet flexible struck his back and the back of his head and turned him round in his fall. Sharp bristles scratched his face and hands as he fell through the branches of a tree, crashing from one to the other before finally rolling semi-conscious onto an unforgiving stone slope. Rolling over and over, bludgeoned by the merciless passage, he tumbled down the foot of the cliff where its sheer wall relented into the valley with a steep curve.

Somehow he was still conscious when he came to a halt, but only hazy vision came to him through a throbbing head. All he could see was the collection of stones nearest him, partially veiled by a cloud of dust from disturbed rocks. Blood poured from his lips, knuckles and elbows, his robes were tattered as if savaged by a pack of wild-cats and every square inch of body screamed with agony. He tried to move but could not. He lay unmoving for a little while before sounds started to register. Dimly he heard gruff voices yammering urgently, and footsteps crunching the loose stones near him. Suddenly he was hauled upright by some monstrous strength and he found himself looking at a fearsome squat-faced figure, like a grotesque statue come to life. Others were nearby, and they fell upon the fallen armists like vultures. There was nothing he could do to resist, but just then, he felt himself falling again as the harrack that had picked him up crumpled to the ground. Lancoir had tackled him like a charging bull, and now scrabbled in the dust with him. How the Captain of the Guard had emerged from the fall with any kind of ability to fight was beyond Roujeark. But now, ferocious as a banshee, Lancoir gained the upper hand and used his heavy boots to crush the brawny figure into the ground. Rising with a whirl he took up a huge stone and smashed it into the face of another harrack. Out of the corner of his eye, Roujeark saw Sin-Serin fighting also, leaping like a gazelle and slashing with daggers, and one or two others, but then he had to concentrate on evading the stamping boot of another harrack. Rolling in the dust with excruciating pain, he tried to get away from the fighting, losing sight of the embattled Lancoir. He heard scuffling feet, blows connecting with sickening crunches, and the thud of falling bodies. When firm hands grasped his shoulders, he feared the worst, but it was Lancoir again, heaving him to his feet and propelling him upward and away.

Making the most of some miraculous opening, they fled the scene. Staggering round an outthrust spine of the cliff, they hobbled into some dead ground. Behind them, the sounds of fighting grew dimmer. A solitary harrack followed them, brandishing a mattock, and Lancoir had just the presence of mind to trip him, casting Roujeark off to one side as he did so. Brutally, he leapt upon his fallen foe and grappled with him. He tried to throttle his enemy, but the harrack's neck was as thick as an ox's haunch, and even more unyielding. The harrack picked up a rock and smashed it into Lancoir's face, knocking him out flat. The knight lay sprawled, unmoving. Slowly, creaking like an old cart, the stocky figure rose and turned his attention to Roujeark. Still woozy, Roujeark felt a surge of fear and panic, but then new adrenaline pumped into him and took over. He flung a stone at the harrack, and in the momentary pause he leaned down and grasped Lancoir's sword, which still lay in its scabbard. Tugging it free just as the harrack was on him, he swung it clumsily and scored it across the thick leather jerkin. It made no more impression than a thin cut, and it did not deter the harrack from coming again. Roujeark was too slow with his swing this time, and a thickly muscled arm punched into his forearm. Yelping with pain, he lost his balance and dropped the sword. Another meaty blow connected with his sternum and he crashed onto his back.

Struggling for breath, and tasting blood in his mouth, Roujeark felt helpless as the horrid figure retrieved his fallen mattock and came to loom over him. The harrack leaned down and seized his robe with a gravelly fist, pulling him up. Up close, Roujeark was appalled by the sight, and the smell. The skin, if you could call it that, was cracked and leathery, and so thin and drawn that it looked like too little skin had been stretched over a skull much too big. The eyes were brutish, but not stupid, and set in an expressionless face that might have been daubed on stone for all the life there was in it. Even as he took in these ghastly details, his smarting fingers were scrabbling desperately for the fallen sword. His fingers locked on it just as the mattock was drawn back for a killing smash. Roujeark swung the sword up, pommel first, and caught the harrack a ringing blow on the cheek. There was a resounding crack. The sparsely lashed eyes blinked curiously, and Roujeark hit him again. Capitalising on the precious advantage, Roujeark shoved up with all his might and helped the stunned harrack topple backwards. Groaning and struggling to get up again, Roujeark leapt upon him and smashed the big pommel-stone down again and again, like a frenzied stone-carver. He kept smiting until the unfamiliar weapon clattered free from his numb grip.

He looked down, appalled at the lifeless mess he had made. Sickened, he pushed himself away. Just then he heard Lancoir stirring. Somehow finding his feet, the ragged knight stumbled forward.

'I...must...help...others...' he mumbled. Summoning his final strength, Roujeark lurched over and grasped his retreating ankle. It was just enough to pitch Lancoir onto his hands and knees. Roujeark crawled up and tried to pin him down. But neither of them had any strength left. So there they lay, battered, broken, barely alive, and not knowing what had become of their companions.

III

Faudunum

COLD. The floor beneath him was so cold. He could hear nothing, see nothing, smell nothing; the only sense he had was touch, the rigid embrace of the ground. Had he been lying there so long that it had seeped deep into his bones, settling in with a deadly ache? There was no mattress, nor even any straw, just unforgiving stone. And it was dark. Impenetrably dark. Curillian tried to lift his head, only to be rewarded with waves of groggy pain that threatened to engulf him in oblivion again. His reward for the effort was to discover than he could in fact see nothing, not even the merest suggestion of light. He tried to stave off unconsciousness, but the freezing cold weight of it was irresistible. Slumping back down, he sank back into dark dreams.

Weightless, unsupported, he saw the gorge again and again. Poised in mid-air, he was condemned to a constant re-evaluation of his decision to cut the bridge. Sometimes he was gazing almost peacefully at the serene peaks away in the distance, sometimes he was looking straight down into the ravine. Sometimes he saw his enemies falling, sometimes his friends. The remorseless dream seemed determined to play before him every possible way in which the scene might have played out. Sometimes he caught hold of the rope before it vanished, sometimes he didn't. Once he saw the sword reach out, almost of its own accord, and wedge itself into the wooden planks just before they fell away, but most times it remained frozen at the end of its fateful last swing. Then he would be falling, always falling…

The impact never came. But when he awoke again on the cold floor, he felt its aftermath. The pain wracked his body, and he did not even know where to begin inspecting his hurts. At least he was more alert this time – or had his previous waking been just another path in his dreams? It seemed familiar, though: unremitting dark and freezing cold. His head throbbed with an awful ache, but at least he felt his thoughts coming clearly to him. Now as well as feeling the cold stone, he was able to discern a dreadful smell, if not its source. He might not be able to see even the walls of his cell, but he knew for sure that cell it was. He knew he was in Faudunum. Nowhere else south of the Haunted Pass could be so cold or so unwelcoming. But he had no idea how he had come here, much less an answer for any of the other questions that queued up in his mind.

He tried again to get up, but his body wouldn't obey. He was still flat on his back when a metal scrape sawed across the silence. The sound startled him, and he looked over to where the sound had come from. A red bar of light emerged, feeble but bright enough to hurt his eyes after all that time in complete darkness. A torch was held up to a small aperture of some kind, and in its flickering, he glimpsed a pale face looking into the cell. He saw the curiosity in the gaze. He saw a part of the wall, and the outline of a huge door. Then the torch withdrew hastily, and the metal plate grated shut again. All the faint outlines he had seen at once melted back into the blackness.

Curillian was unable to measure the passing hours, but some time later he was able to haul himself into a sitting position, numbed muscles cramping with the sudden effort. Gradually he managed to stand up and, once standing, he patted himself all over to discover what state he was in. Though bereft of the warm outer cloak the snow-elves had given him, he was dressed in all the same clothes.

A chain pendant from Carmen still hung about his neck. His other effects were gone, though. His pack had been taken, together with all his provisions. Feeling round his belt, he found his dagger gone, and, worst of all, his great blade. The Sword of Maristonia was in the hands of harracks! Wretched as he was, the thought burned in him like acid in his stomach.

With nothing else to do, he investigated his cell also. He stumbled blindly in search of the nearest wall. Locating it with an outstretched hand, he paced around the cell. He found only two features to break the otherwise square perimeter. His nose warned him by the smell before he came to the small, sloped orifice in one corner. There could be no doubt of its purpose: a latrine had been provided, not so much for his convenience as to spare the guards the need to clean his cell. Nauseated, he lurched to the other wall and found the sloping indent which was the second feature. He thought this was where the light had come from, and, sure enough, as his fingers groped out, they touched something even colder than the stone. Metal. It was the plate sealing the spyhole, but he could not move it, nor find any handle or lever.

He jumped back when it moved from the other side. Again, the sudden light of the torch was dazzling, and he held up a hand to block it out. When he removed his fingers, he saw the same face looking in at him. Its eyes looked surprised to see him so close by. They were not the eyes of a harrack. They were elven, set in a pale smooth face. Immediately Curillian thought of what Sin-Serin had told him, about one of Aiiyosha's folk who had gone missing near Faudunum. Was this he? The voice too, when it spoke, was elven.

'So, you are up. I have been eager to speak with you.'

'Who is it that wishes to speak with me?' Curillian was shocked by how hoarse his voice was – he scarcely recognised the sound of himself.

'One who knows who you are, so do not waste your time in denying it.'

'And who am I?'

'The King of Maristonia, Curillian the Mighty. A catch of singular value...'

'That's an ambitious guess. The harracks...?'

'The harracks also know who you are. They might not be the most perspicacious of creatures, but they never forget a sword like yours, one that has done them so much damage in the past. Do you deny it?'

'I do not deny it. And yet I thought I'd done enough damage to the barbarians for them to have no hesitation in killing me. Why have they not done so?'

'I convinced them not to.'

'Why? They must know they'd never be able to ransom me. Or do they simply delay to prepare a slow death for me?'

'You're probably right about the ransom, though it would be interesting to watch them try. The loss in prestige to your house alone would be incalculable. And yes, given half a chance, they would take great delight in subjecting you to the tortures of the deep. But I have persuaded them otherwise...for now...and I had another reason for so doing.'

'What reason?'

'I believe you possess information which would be very useful to me.'

Curillian shot forward, pressing his face close to the open grate. The person on the other side stepped hastily back, casting torchlight over the rough passage outside. He was swathed in warm furs, but the stature of the snow-elves was unmistakeable, very similar to Aiiyosha.

'And who are you that guesses?' Curillian demanded. 'An elf, certainly, and most likely a snow-elf. But whoever you are, I will not converse through a hole!'

'King of armists, it may be the hole or nothing. Perhaps I was too quick to rouse you and should have left you a little while longer for the cell to cool your ardour. At least be willing to eat and drink what is passed through the hole.' Curillian brought his hands up and objects were placed in them. 'I will return soon,' the elf said. '...when, I hope, you will be more amenable.'

The grate snapped shut, but in the last second of light Curillian saw what had been given to him. He was amazed to see a flask and a hunk of bread from his pack. Amazed, he slumped down against the wall and tore hungrily at the food and slurped the water down. All too soon it was gone, and then he was left alone with his thoughts in the darkness.

⋏

With great caution, Roujeark and Lancoir made their way back to the scene of the fallen bridge. They peered from behind a concealing rock for a long time before feeling sure that no harracks were about. Then, apprehensively, they emerged from hiding. Nursing their bruised and aching limbs, they crept down the rocky slope and out into the flat open space of the gorge's bottom. The scene was carnage. Broken lengths of the bridge lay draped over stones like so much firewood. Roujeark looked up and was astonished to see how high the ravine's sides looked from below. There, waving gently like bones in a drafty tomb, were the broken ends of the bridge, hanging from either cliff face. Looking down again, the humps they had seen proved to be just what they had feared: bodies, half-buried in dust and fragmented rock. Ignoring the fallen harracks, they hurriedly identified those which were armists: five of them. Lancoir pulled them free one by one and turned them over to see their faces.

'Cyron...Edrist...Norscinde...Caréysin...Andil.' He called out their names mournfully and wept over them.

The last three were still breathing faintly, and Roujeark was relieved to see his friend Andil among them. He and Caréysin seemed more or less unharmed, just stunned, but Cyron and Edrist were unmoving. Norscinde was conscious, but when his dim eyes looked up, Lancoir was only able to see the life draining from him. The knight clasped the dying armist's hand until it went limp.

Roujeark sat helplessly by, wracked by grief but too exhausted for tears. The three guardsmen had seemingly been killed by the fall, their backs and necks broken like twigs. All they could do for them was to straighten out their crooked limbs and pile cairns of stones over them. Caréysin and Andil they revived as best they could, though both were injured. As they were doing so, the sound of rocks being disturbed startled them. Lancoir dropped the stone in his hand and reached for his sword, and Roujeark prepared a rock for throwing. There, trudging across the stony watercourse, was Lionenn, the Konenaire. So covered in dust and rocky debris was he that he looked like a corpse risen from some mountain tomb. Limping with a wound in one leg, he came up to them and rested upon the great harrack mattock he bore.

'Lionenn? Where have you come from?' Lancoir said in gruff welcome. The grizzled armist was no less gruff in reply.

'Killing harracks. Lost my bloody axe. Catching the last one took me away yonder.' He gestured stiffly up the valley. 'Bastard smashed my leg with this club, but I smashed his head. Bastard.' He spat out dust and blood but weighed the mattock approvingly. Lancoir smiled grimly and thumped his arm.

'Good armist. We should have brought a few more Konenaires,' he said. No sooner had he finished speaking than a new sound came from across the river. A figure was stumbling down towards them from the scree slope at the far side of the gorge. It was not a harrack. It was an armist.

'Aleinus!?' Lancoir said in amazement. The guard in question fell to his knees, sobbing uncontrollably and clasping his hands in front of him as if in prayer. They helped him up and he joined them in burying their comrades. When asked how he survived, he told his story in the fragments that came to him.

'I was at the front, near the king. When he cut through the bridge, I flung myself forward to try and catch him, but his momentum took him sideways and instead of reaching him I just managed to grab the other half of the bridge as it fell away. That meant I ended up on the other side of the gorge, away from the rest of you. When the harracks fell around me I just managed to hold on, having gained a good grip. I just hung there, not able to do anything. Eventually I could hold on no longer, and I fell. I expected the impact to kill me, but instead I must have been knocked out. When I woke up again, the ground beneath me was somehow softer than rock. It took me a while to realise that I'd landed on a pile of dead harracks. They're hard enough, though, jolting pains were shooting up my back. Even now, every movement is agony. I waited, in the shadow of the cliff, hoping against hope. When I saw you…I can't tell you…' He broke down again, tears coursing through the dust caked on his face. Roujeark laid a comforting hand on his shoulder.

'So you're alive, and we're alive,' said Lancoir slowly. 'That makes five, but where are the rest?' Together they searched the floor of the gorge desperately. Through waves of pain, they were overjoyed to uncover two more bodies half-hidden by the stones. They could scarcely believe it when they found that both bodies belonged to live armists. Utarion and Antaya were just coming around from deep concussions. They were even more battered than the rest of them, but somehow, they had survived the fall in one piece. They kept searching in growing desperation. They turned up fallen packs, but no more bodies did they find.

'There's no sign of the king,' Roujeark said, voicing the thought troubling all of them.

'I wish someone saw everything, someone who could tell us what the hell happened.' Lancoir spoke into his hands as they massaged his weary face.

'I don't remember much. I was dazed, and everything happened so quickly. I remember harracks attacking us, and I think I saw Sin-Serin alive and fighting, but it was only a glimpse,' Roujeark recollected with difficulty.

Aleinus was little help. 'Everything had happened by the time I came to. The gorge was empty when I regained my senses. Nothing happened until you two came back...'

'I can barely say more,' said Lancoir, looking at Roujeark. 'How I got up at all I'll never know, but when I saw you being attacked, I was up before I knew what I was doing.' He rubbed his wounded shoulder as he recalled tackling the harrack which had picked Roujeark up. Roujeark slotted this memory into his own and fingered the ring Lancoir had given him. He looked at it, covered in dust, but unbroken. the debt was repaid, if nothing else. Suddenly he became aware that Lancoir was berating himself.

'I should have stayed. My first thought was to get you to safety, out of harm's way. I thought that once I'd done that I could return in good conscience. But I never made it back...'

Roujeark tried to comfort him.

'You had no strength left, and there was nothing you could have done anyway...' Lancoir swatted his hand aside, and rose, suddenly furious.

'But I left the king! I shoulder never have left the king.' He shouted the words and they echoed off the gorge walls. Wincing, he lowered his voice. 'I abandoned him, and now he's either dead or captive. I shall offer my life in penance, if only I can find him again.'

His shout reminded them that they were all in terrible danger out there in the open. Roujeark was just about to usher them back into cover when they heard a moaning. Fearing attack again, they prepared to defend themselves, but all that happened was more moaning. It seemed to come from the trees. They staggered back up into the trees, following the noise, and found a body dangling from the lower branches of a fir tree. Incoherent with pain, it was another live armist. It was Findor, the last of their ill-fated company. As gently as they could, they lowered him down, and then took stock of things. Hidden for the moment by the trees, they allowed themselves a rest. They took on water and food salvaged from the shattered packs.

Lancoir, Roujeark, Andil, Caréysin, Aleinus and Lionenn were all battered and bruised, but they could move unaided. Antaya was able to get up with some assistance, Findor lay groaning in pain, but Utarion was unable to move. Apparently only his eyes and lips were still active. They laid him on his back, devastated by his pitiful condition. His fingers scrabbled by his side, and, following his gaze, Lancoir placed his sword in his hand. The inert guard grasped it weakly, and then murmured to his captain. Lancoir held his other hand tightly, watching as he slowly expired. There were no more tears to come from the exhausted captain, but the pain disfigured his face as he complied with his comrade's last request. His passing did not take long, and at the end there was peace in his face. They covered him with stones like the others. Then Antaya, who prized his faith, and honoured that of his fallen comrades, spoke words of prayer and farewell over the sad little cairns.

It was a pathetic, dishevelled little company that left the cover of the trees and struck out across the gorge. They went at a slow, limping pace, the best they could manage with their collective injuries. Its shell-shocked members proceeded with little clear idea of where they were going, and with even less hope, but Lancoir led them forward with his slowly recovering strength. Wearily, painfully, they inched along the far wall of the gorge, feeling as small as ants, and following it blindly in the hope that it led somewhere. They came to a deep fold in the cliff-face and the sound of stones being disturbed made them all freeze with fear. Fumbling for weapons, they looked up a steep slope, seeing nothing at first. Then, with extraordinary slowness, a statue-like figure became outlined against the rocky backdrop. The figure was kneeling, bowstring pulled back taut. Gradually Sin-Serin became recognisable, as if she had temporarily been part of the cliff itself and now came back to life.

'Falakai,' she breathed softly to herself in relief. Marvelling at her camouflage, their fears dissipated. The tension eased with her bowstring, and then, incongruously, she smiled down at them.

'Well met, friends. I'm glad to see you still alive. But come, our mission is not over; far from it, it is now harder than ever. If you think surviving this far was hard, think not of what lies before you. Let us beseech Prélan that he spares you also through what comes next. Come. Follow me...'

W hen his visitor came again, Curillian thought he now had some idea of how to play things. He seated himself with his back to the far wall, facing the aperture. When the faint red light came through and illuminated him, it revealed a very composed figure.

'Well, king of armists, I hope you will make my visit more worthwhile this time. I doubt I shall be able to come alone many more times...' Curillian stretched out the silence before answering levelly.

'I may know something which would be valuable to you...' His benign interrogator waited expectantly. 'But why should I tell it to you...?'

'To spare yourself worse treatment,' came back the hasty response, obviously prepared. Curillian scoffed.

'You must do better than that, snow-elf. Don't take me for a fool. The harracks will kill me one way or another. You must give me a reason to loosen my tongue...' This time his questioner took longer to respond.

'I...may be able to help you,' he said hesitantly. 'But I cannot tell you how without knowing what it is you offer.'

Looking up from where he sat, Curillian could not see the snow-elf; he was just talking to the red slit in the opposite wall. He smiled to himself.

'Why don't I tell you how you could help me?' he said, long practice infusing his voice with more confidence than he felt. His questioner paused, unsure of this proposal. 'You can take me to the elf-woman held captive here.'

'Impossible!' the voice on the other side of the wall hissed quickly. 'I cannot just go guiding you round the dungeons...'

Curillian smiled inwardly again. So, she is here. He waited, sensing the indecision behind the snow-elf's refusal.

'She is held in a deep cell, far from here. It would be extremely difficult to access, and even harder to do so undetected. You would have to know something very valuable for so much trouble...'

'I'm sure you would like to know why I am really in these mountains,' Curillian offered. 'I'm even more sure that the harracks would. What's more, I think you knowing such a thing would give you great credit with your friends...'

Curillian wished he could see the other's face as he spoke, gauge the reaction, but even talking to a wall he could sense the temptation and uncertainty. He held his breath. There was silence for a long while, but then the metal panel was scraped shut and footsteps retreated down the passage outside.

Curillian got up and paced around. He needed to keep his mind active and focused, lest madness start to creep in. Whoever this elf was, there was a reason why he and not the harracks were attending to him. An elf would not reside easily in a place such as Faudunum, so he must have some use, or render some service to the harracks. Curillian felt sure, though, that he was a duplicitous character, trying to play both sides. The very fact that he was contemplating assisting a prisoner showed that he was willing to damage the harracks' cause. Or at least, so it seemed. He had admitted that Carea was here, and even if he didn't know who she was, he must know how valuable a prisoner she was from how secure cell she was kept in. His outright refusal to go near her had changed very quickly to a willingness to bargain. Whatever his agenda was, whatever it was he wanted, he wanted it badly. But how badly? Curillian felt sure he would come back, but he hoped it wouldn't be too long. He must play this just right, for this snow-elf might be his best chancing of escaping. The thought of being trapped in the darkness of Faudunum for the rest of his days didn't bear thinking about. Already even just losing the pathetic red light from the viewing hole had made his heart sink. He must get out, and soon…

A

Now with Sin-Serin leading them, the battered little company of nine continued on its way. After a long trek, they rounded the sharp end of the great ridge which filled the wider valley. Beyond it, the far side of the valley rose up as a long steep wall. Welcoming the thick mists that had come over, they trudged up that steep valley-side. After a wearisome climb, they emerged out of the mists which filled the valley and found themselves on a rough, barren plateau. It proved to be quite narrow though, for they soon came to its far side. There they were brought up short by another obstacle, and another breath-taking spectacle.

It seemed that they were on the roof of the world, looking down upon it. Again, the ground fell away before them in sudden precipitous cliffs and plunged to unguessable depths. To either side they heard the trickle of little streams falling into the abyss, only to be blown away in fine spray. Across from them, many miles away, they saw another area of high ground, which seemed to be the same height upon which they now stood, only curved round like a horseshoe. All the vast gap in between was filled with mist, as if it were a cauldron containing mysterious vapours. Yet out of that great emptiness rose a peak, its sides as sheer as the cliffs at their feet but flat enough at the summit to accommodate a forbidding fortress. Squat, crude and grey, the fort sat foursquare on that improbable pinnacle, seeming almost to float above the sea of mist. They were left in no doubt as to its ownership. Even from this distance they could see sentries as squat and hard as the fastness itself: harracks. Nor were they just perched in the building, like would-be eagles in a hand-built eyrie: they also manned what looked to be the only approach to the high place. A ludicrously steep staircase, hewn out of the living rock, climbed up to the fortress. The steps were broken every now and then by a level of flat rock where sentries skulked. Leaning over as far as they dared, they saw a knife-thin bridge of living rock emerge from under the cliff on which they stood and stretch across the yawning mists to the fortified crag.

All this they saw with mixed dread and wonderment.

'Cor, would you look at that place?' exclaimed Antaya. 'Can you imagine having to attack it?'

None of them wanted to, and with one mind they pushed the thought aside. Instead, their attentions fixated on where to go next. The steep staircase vanished into the mist after a few of the level places, giving no clues as to what lurked below; nor could they see any way down from their present position. They crouched down in congress to consider things.

'We were indeed fortunate not to come this way originally,' declared Sin-Serin. 'Aiiyosha told us that this is where the right-hand turn in the lower valley would have led us.'

'So somewhere down there is a gap which would lead us back to where we started,' Roujeark observed.

'A straighter road,' agreed Lancoir. 'But it would have brought us right to their door-step.'

'The question is where to go now,' Roujeark told them.

'Can we bypass this fort?' Caréysin asked.

'Perhaps,' said Sin-Serin. 'My guess is that there is a path which leads from this outpost to the main stronghold of Faudunum. Somehow we must get down to that path, but without being seen. Let us hope we have not been descried already upon this height.' Roujeark shivered with that thought, drawing his cloak tight about his aching shoulders. Lancoir was already up and ready to move.

'Come; let us find what way we can. One thing is certain: however we get to Faudunum, the longer we take, the less chance we have of finding the king alive when we get there...'

The metal scraped again, breaking the silence, and the red light appeared again. Curillian had been expecting the third visit, but all the same, he was relieved when it came. The aching still throbbed all over his body, but he forced himself to concentrate.

'Does my visitor have a name?' he called out.

'Perethor,' the voice came back. *Perethor,* Curillian echoed thoughtfully to himself. *And who is Perethor?*

'And what is a snow-elf doing in Faudunum?' was what he asked out loud.

'I will ask the questions,' Perethor snapped. 'What are you doing in Stonad?' Curillian broke in, keeping him off balance.

'I know who you are,' he declared, taking his questioner aback. 'You are of the clan of Aiiyosha, whose hospitality we have just enjoyed. She told us that one of her kinsmen went missing, near to Faudunum...that kinsman is you, isn't it Perethor?' He got no answer, but he knew he was right. He spoke his thoughts aloud. 'I thought we might be able to rescue you, but maybe you don't want to return to your kin?'

A nerve was struck.

'I would do anything to live among my people again.' Perethor's voice was sharp and bitter. 'Do not judge me or make guesses about me, armist; what would you know of exile?'

A rush of memories swept up from hidden places to engulf Curillian. *All too much.* His jaw clenched, but he stayed calm, and the moment passed.

'Actually, my friend, I know as much about exile as anyone alive. I know what it is to be deprived of hearth and home and honour.' He got up and walked to the red slit. He wanted to see Perethor's face for this. The snow-elf did not like having him closer, but he stood his ground. He seemed to be in the grip of some strong emotion. 'Were you driven,' Curillian asked gently, 'or did you run?'

Perethor grimaced. 'What does it matter now? I came here, and here was I snared. You have been a captive here for two days, armist king, but I have been a captive for many circuits of the sun.' Compassion rose in Curillian.

'I will help you if you help me.' Perethor looked at him sharply.

'Do you really know something that would buy us both our freedom?'

'Yes,' said Curillian. 'I believe I do. But how can I trust you?'

'That is a chance you must take. If you have not guessed it already, both our lives are at stake. The harrack has no more love for the traitor than for the trespasser. Come, what is this knowledge you possess?' Curillian hesitated, weighing up the rightness of what he was about to say.

'Would I be right in thinking that the harracks are desperate to strike a blow at their lowland enemies?' Perethor nodded, waiting. 'What if I were to tell you that they might soon have an opportunity to strike at many enemies?' His conscience pricked him even as he said the words, but he felt he had no choice. Perethor's eyes widened with interest.

'Truly? Where?' Curillian smiled thinly.

'I will say no more until you release me. Get me out of here, and we shall talk again.' It was Perethor's turn to hesitate. He stood there, transfixed with indecision. Curillian watched many emotions go across his face. He willed him to a positive decision; his heart rose within him when he seemed to reach inside his robes for a set of keys, and then his hopes were dashed as he reached out a hand and slammed the viewing hole plate shut. The metal clanged in front of Curillian's nose and he heard shoes slapping hurriedly against the stone floor, beating a hasty retreat. He struck the walls with his fists and cursed aloud to the darkness in his frustration. He had been so close...

A

Roujeark didn't know how they managed it, but eventually they found a way down. Not before several of them had nearly fallen to their deaths, not before countless slips and twisted ankles, not before hours of bone-chilled toil, but eventually they found a way. They clambered down a slope so steep that Roujeark would have sworn beforehand that it could not be scaled. Without the ropes in their packs, and close co-operation between them, they never would have made it. Every minute spent clinging to that wind-buffeted rock-face, scrabbling for handholds and places to rest his feet, felt like an hour. More than once, he nearly slipped into misty oblivion, and the others fared little better.

Their luck had nearly given out when they had drawn near the level of the bridge that connected the cliff with the outcrop. A sudden noise, as of deep horns blowing, came from within the fort and startled them so that they nearly lost their grips. All of them came to a halt and clung to the cliff as best they could. Those that were able to watched as the fort's great doors were flung open, and out of them issued a column of harracks. Perhaps forty in number, they came tramping out of the fort with heavy booted feet. All were armoured with chainmail and leather and pointed iron caps, and all bore sturdy shields and thick, short spears. Over everything, they were swathed in thick black bear-skins, in which they very quickly seemed to meld into the night as soon as they had left behind the glare of the watch-torches. Yet they gave no sign that they had seen the armists, but followed the bridge to the cliff-face, where they picked up a steep path descending down into the valley. The doors of the fort were slammed behind them, and noisily they marched away, chanting war songs in deep throaty voices.

The company waited until the harrack patrol was gone and then resumed their descent. With bruised and bleeding fingers barely able to relax from their clenched gripping positions, they eventually managed to get down. Roujeark would have liked to rest, but Lancoir drove them on mercilessly. Until he could get back to his king, he was like an armist possessed. Riding their luck, they hurried across a broken valley floor and splashed over a narrow stream. The heights above from which they had descended were lost to view.

'This must be the upper reaches of Pharaphir,' said Sin-Serin. 'Prélan be praised that her waters are cleansed from harrack filth ere they reach the forest. Come, let us be swift and gain the cover of those trees ahead. Danger is all around.'

Half-running, half-stumbling, nearly blind with weariness, they followed her suggestion and came to the trees. It was a narrow stand of fir trees. The cover offered was thin, but it was better than nothing. They paused briefly, and then went on. Creeping now, they cautiously approached the far side of the stand. From the far trees, they could see a rough-beaten road running alongside.

'That road must link the fortress we passed with Faudunum,' Lancoir guessed. 'At least we now know the way.'

Roujeark seized his arm fearfully. 'But how will we escape their notice, being so close?' Lancoir smiled grimly at him, the smile known only to veterans of a hundred campaigns.

'We must hope they are looking the other way!'

They carried on, full of fear, expecting discovery any moment. Their pace of march was the best compromise they could manage between a desire for speed on the one hand, and the need to be as quiet as possible on the other. They might have gone quicker, but their tortured bodies slowed them down with grating pain. All of them were fortunate to be mobile at all. Several times Sin-Serin, leading again, had them down flat on their bellies when she suspected some danger. Caréysin kept an arrow ready on the string while all the rest of them watched Sin-Serin's shadowy outline in the gloom. She would have them wait, faces pressed to the pine-needle-covered ground, for interminable ages before she judged that the danger had passed. None of the rest of them could guess what made her fearful, but on the last occasion, they were still lying flat when they heard the faint thrum of heavy feet. Not daring to move a muscle, hardly daring to breathe, they waited in agonising tension as the booted feet came nearer. Glancing up, Roujeark just made out a patrol of ten or so harracks stomping down the road. They were dressed and armoured like the other patrol, but now they were close enough for him to see that above their huge boots were strange greaves and gaiters of fur. He felt certain they would turn aside and find them, but their stride never faltered. They kept going; back down the valley in the direction of the fortress.

Gradually they eased up and got going again, but it was not long before Sin-Serin had them down on one knee again. Roujeark's heart started to thud again, but this time their elven guide gestured through the trees. She pointed out a hill up ahead, rising out of the valley. Manoeuvring into a better position, Roujeark could see what she was pointing out. The bleak hill was crowned with a fell citadel. Low, crumpled and gnarled, the city ran around the brow of the hill like an iron circlet. It looked more like a grave-ring than a habitation of the living. The path beside them ran up to it, flanked all the way by trees. Red torches flickering above the gates were the only evidence of colour in all that mass of grey. They could see their destination, but could they get to it...?

⚊

Curillian knelt in prayer. Ignoring the discomfort of his posture, he poured out his heart to Prélan.

O merciful Father, do not abandon me here in this darkness! How long will You let me languish here? The days merge into one and are as night to me. My hope falters within me. Yet I remember You, the God of my youth. Ever were You faithful to me, and always You preserved my life against my enemies. Arise now in strength, and deliver me from my foes. Fill this tired and aching body with new strength, and give me what it takes to reclaim my freedom. Grant that I might bring Carea out with me, and continue on my quest...

The words melted into the darkness and fled before him. No answer came, only that familiar inward peace. Lying down and closing his eyes, sleep took him again, one darkness replacing another.

The scraping of the key in the lock startled him awake. He opened his eyes, not that it made any difference. He had lost track of time, so he did not know whether hours or days had passed since he had scared Perethor off, but now something was definitely going on outside. It was not the viewing-hole – this scuffling was coming from the door. Ignoring the ropes of pain in his back and the howls of complaints from his knees and elbows, he eased up into a crouch, tense and ready for action. He heard, rather than saw, the door open. In a few quick strides, he was across the cell. Cannoning into the barely open door, he threw his weight against it and heaved it ajar, letting the red light from the corridor spill into the cell. In doing so, he knocked over Perethor, who was just unbending from the keyhole. With the catlike reflexes of an elf, Perethor was up again, darting to block Curillian's escape. Curillian had intended to take only a split second to take stock of his new surroundings, but the torchlight was dazzling after so long in the darkness and his eyes smarted. Gradually he got the measure of the corridor, which was low and narrow. Perethor could not stand fully upright, but had to stoop. He realised there was only one exit, and the elf was now between him and it, tensed ready for trouble.

'Don't even think about running, armist king. You won't get anywhere if you break faith with me. All I have to do is shout and harrack guards will be upon you.' Curillian stared levelly at him.

'It'd already be too late for you if you did. How did I get out of my cell, they'll want to know.' Perethor had no answer; he knew he was right. Curillian made it doubly clear for him. 'No, you stand complicit now, and you won't get me back in that cell without one of us dying. We need each other.' The elf relaxed almost imperceptibly.

'Well then, I have released you. Now tell me what you know.' Curillian shook his head.

'Take me to the elf-woman first.'

'That wasn't our agreement.'

'It is now. You take me to her, or you'll get nothing from me.' Perethor looked desperate. He wavered, and Curillian rushed at him. The elf was quick, but Curillian was quicker, and in a flash he had his accomplice pinned against the wall. 'Take me to her, Perethor. You need me now more than I need you. I can take your keys and find her on my own, but you need what I know, or they'll show you no mercy.'

He was bluffing – he doubted he would find Carea at all, let alone in time before he was caught – but he infused his voice with all the aggression and confidence he could muster to keep Perethor from realising it.

'I've never seen her...' Perethor prevaricated.

'But you know where her cell is. Take me there.' Still the elf dithered, his courage deserting him. Curillian thrust his face close. Desperation gave his voice a ruthless edge. 'I've never killed an elf before, but believe me, with these bare hands I'll tear your head off if you don't do as I say.' Perethor resisted a moment longer, and then buckled.

'All right, all right,' he whimpered. 'But for pity's sake we must be quick.'

He wriggled out of Curillian's grasp and shuffled, wincing, to the door at the end of the corridor. He placed another key in the lock, turned it with impeccable care, and then looked over his shoulder at Curillian.

'Make any noise more than a patter, and we're dead.'

With oily speed, he inched open the door and vanished through it. Curillian made haste to follow. Evidently knowing the way very well, Perethor scurried down the eerily-lit passageways like a rabbit, but as stealthily as a cat. It was all Curillian could do to keep up. Only briefly were they exposed in the inhabited parts, and after that, they were flying down dim corridors of stone to another clutch of dungeons. Deeper and deeper they went, and the way became tighter and narrower as they went. Eventually, panting and alive with nervous energy, Perethor came to a halt in a low tunnel. He paused at a corner, and peered round.

'Good, there is no guard here,' he whispered in relief.

'Is there normally?'

'No, we are so deep now that none are needed. There is no way out of here except back the way we came. We were fortunate, though, not to run into any guards on the higher levels...' That thought seemed to trouble him, but he pushed it away and slipped round the corner, whisking Curillian with him. In this last section, the tunnel got so low that they had to stoop almost double. At its end was a portal, small but sturdy, and fastened with many locks. It looked almost airtight. Perethor turned to Curillian again.

'Well, here we are, just as you asked. Now make good your end of the bargain.' Curillian shook his head.

'Not yet, I need to see her, make sure she's alive.' Perethor looked aggrieved, and, very suddenly, like he was on the brink of breaking down completely. Curillian reasoned with him. 'If I tell you now, what's to stop you dashing off and leaving me here? The information would save your skin, but I'd be doomed.' He saw the fear and rising terror in the elf's eyes. With a will, he hardened his heart and kept his resolve. He gripped Perethor's arm, and looked him deep in the eye.

'I will not abandon you, friend Perethor. One way or another, I will get you out of this city. Now, open this up.'

Trembling, Perethor opened the locks one by one, and then turned a small wheel in the portal's centre. Each turn of the wheel relaxed the pent-up tension of the barrier further until, at last, it swung open with a gasp of released air. Cold, clammy air wafted into Curillian's nose. His heart thudded with foreboding, and a sudden hesitation seized him. Perethor was even more unwilling. He cringed away from the mysterious opening, as if mortally afraid of it.

'I will not go in,' he murmured. Curillian overcame his hesitation and crammed himself through the opening. It was barely big enough for him. As he squeezed through, he heard Perethor muttering balefully to himself.

'Hurry, hurry, make haste, make haste...'

The opening was actually just one end of a small extension of the tunnel. He fought down the panic of being so enclosed under the earth. Had he only swapped one cell for another? Eventually he scrabbled through, landing on what appeared to be a high shelf. All about him was dark. Not so dark as his former cell – he could just make out the shape of the chamber he was in – but dark enough. The shelf he was on seemed to go all the way around an empty space, hugging the walls near the ceiling. Below, the air fell away into a deep, dank pit. The shelf almost seemed to be a platform for looking down at what was below. He swallowed in horror, to think that a living person should be kept here in the bowels of Faudunum. There was something sinister about that thought that made his own cell seem bearable by comparison. If a prison were to be specially devised for the incarceration of a dangerous shape-shifter, it would be difficult to surpass this place. At first, though, he thought no one was there. He could see nothing, hear nothing, and smell nothing but damp rock.

Had Perethor tricked him, and brought him to the wrong place? He lay still, straining, all too aware of time slipping by and his heart thumping furiously in his chest. At last, he called out.

'Carea?'

He sensed the barest change in the atmosphere, as if the name had hit home somewhere. Straining his eyes, he thought he saw the tiniest movement and a scrape of something light against a dark backdrop. He thought he was seeing things, but then, with painstaking slowness, a piteous figure uncurled itself and stood up on shaky legs. Thin, frail, covered in filth and grime, the identity was nevertheless unmistakeable. The confinement had not subdued the tall elegance yet, nor had the darkness managed to wholly dim the immortal beauty. Just as he and the others had feared, Carea was here. He had never quite fully believed it until now. He shuddered to see the awful reality of her predicament. Had he not come, here she would have remained, her immortality no longer a virtue but a condemnation to eternal bondage. No death would have intervened to cut short her suffering. Choked to tears by these thoughts, it took Curillian several moments to counter them with the realisation that he was here now, and could do something about it. Pushing aside his revulsion, and the nagging thought of how she had come to be here in the first place, he called to her again.

'Carea...' The pale figure stepped unsteadily towards him, looking up with shocked eyes. Her voice came up to him, distant and wondering.

'That voice...I know that voice. My heart remembers those tones. Out of darkness I am transported to rolling green fields where the horses ran strong, to a time of unlikely fellowship, and courageous common cause...' She paused as tears and sorrow overtook her. Her sobs cut through the damp air like whiplashes. Through the grief, she spoke again, welcome words welling up from improbable hope. '… Oh my Ruthion, is it really you…? Are you really here?'

To hear her voice plead so piteously cut him to the heart, laying bare the emotions that had been covered by centuries of forgetting.

'It is. I am here.' He felt more tears coming to his own eyes, and emotion catching in his voice. 'Carea, I've come for you. You're leaving this vile place…now.' He held out his hands, stretching downwards.

'*Prélan étyr lauthaeyes, miel Maren ilyades gevron ídavalir Maray gaälésus hán.*'

She reached up with her arms. She could not reach. Curillian slithered forward, stretching as far as he could. Fleetingly their fingers touched, but they could not grasp the other's hands. Swallowing hard, Curillian swung his legs round and launched himself down into the pit, all his pain forgotten. As soon as he was down, he knelt by her, then reached up for her hands. She understood what he was doing, and placed her feet on his shoulders. She weighed nothing. Trusting the balance of an elf, Curillian heaved upwards, lifting her into the air. He felt her let go of his hands and reach upwards for the shelf.

'I cannot reach…' she cried. A rage took him then. He would not be defeated; he would not let them remain here in this pit. Summoning strength that for all but the most extreme of needs lay well out of reach, he seized her calves, crouched down, and with a pain-filled roar of defiance, he launched her upwards. He felt the miniscule weight leave him. He heard her scrabble against the rock, heard her exertion as she rolled up onto the shelf. Now for him. She could not reach down to him anymore than he had been able to reach down for her, so he rushed to the far side of the pit. He hurled himself back, sprinting across the floor, and leapt up onto the wall. Needing no handholds, his feet ran up the vertical face like steps. His momentum carried him up to her waiting arms, and then she took over before he fell back down. Long imprisonment could not totally atrophy the ancient strength of the noblest race that ever walked beneath the sun, and she lifted him upwards until he could seize the shelf for himself. He hauled himself up, and then lay panting, the extra strength deserting him as quickly as it had risen up.

The urgency of the situation jabbed him like an elbow in the ribs. He forced himself to first sit up, and then crouch. She too crouched, and for a moment, they beheld each other's eyes. What she was thinking, Curillian did not know, but he was gauging her strength. What lay before was surely more difficult and dangerous than what had already passed. She looked so weak, so pale and drawn, that he doubted she could manage shape-shifting or any other magic. He hoped she could run, but he would carry her if he must. He took her hand and yanked her to her feet.

'Come, we must be gone.' He paused at the open portal to whisper through. 'Perethor, we're coming out.'

There was no answer.

When Curillian had crawled back through, he found the elf gone. 'Curse him!' he hissed savagely. 'The coward has deserted us.'

'Who?' Carea asked as Curillian turned to help her through also.

'Perethor, a snow-elf – it was he who led me down here.'

'I do not know him. Only harracks…'

'Come, we cannot worry about him now. If he's fled, he'll be dead soon, and so will we if we don't get out of here. Can you run?'

'My legs will carry me if they must.'

'They must.'

He whisked her away and then they were flying, hand-in-hand, blindly back up the low corridors of Faudunum. Without Perethor he did not know the way, but he retraced their steps as best he could remember. The faithless snow-elf was nowhere to be seen. At any moment he expected the hue and cry to go up. Stealth was still possible, but if the alarm should sound, he knew all they could do was make a run for it. He needed to recover his sword also, but if that were not possible, then Carea was by far the more precious of the two. He would get her out if he could, and then come back for the sword. The tournament could wait; he would not leave the Sword of Maristonia in the hands of heathens.

They saw no one, and with every corner turned, their fears redoubled. Cold sweat ran in chilling drops down his spine. At last, they seemed to come to the upper levels. Curillian fought to control his breathing as Carea collapsed against him. Her weakened legs gave way beneath her. He would have to support her from now on.

He led her out into a grey corridor where receding daylight told him that evening had fallen. They passed the nightmarish shapes of harrack carvings that leered at them in the half-light. With Curillian half-supporting, half-carrying the princess, they staggered along the corridor, their feet slapping against the stones. They passed the misshapen apertures of a miserable cloister, but no sign of life did they see in the hard courtyard beyond. Curillian's suspicions began to grow. He was about to lead her out towards the open sky, thinking that way offered their best hope, when his way was blocked by falling stone crashing down in front of his toes. He leapt back and tangled with Carea, the pair of them falling in a heap. The building itself remained standing, but stone barriers, moved by some cunning of the harrack masons, fell down over the cloister apertures. He blinked through the dust – he had never seen anything like it. Were the harracks able to manipulate stone like a potter would clay? He picked them up, and stumbled in another direction, the only one which had been left open to them. Up some stairs they limped, and then, again, when they tried to turn in a promising direction, they were brought up short by stone angrily reforming into a barricade. Were they being watched, their way barred only when they came to a favourable route? He felt like a mouse trapped in a changing labyrinth, but he struggled on.

They made their way heavily along another tunnel, hoping for another glimpse of open air. If they could only find a way to the battlements, find a postern gate, or something… As they were hobbling along, the floor itself turned against them. The lifeless flagstone lurched up beneath them like a catapult, tipping them off balance. At the same time, a treacherous hole appeared in the wall, which moments before had been solid stone. They were pitched down a long slope and deposited out into another corridor. The burning pain of all Curillian's hurts returned, but he had to pick himself and Carea up again. Another corridor, another turn, another sudden dead end.

Hopelessly disorientated, they saw ruddy light ahead and stumbled up a wide staircase. Suddenly they emerged out into an open space. It was what he had hoped for – a glimpse of the city's outer battlements, and a clear way to reach them – but his hope cheated him. The vast courtyard they had entered was not empty. Through thin nighttime mists, he saw Perethor, and with him were a hundred harracks. Their torches blazed all around, garishly illuminating grim stones and mocking faces alike. The way of escape was blocked by a hundred mattocks and maces, while above them, more harracks stood ready with crossbows and slingshots to shoot them down.

The wretched snow-elf looked terrified, and well he might, for next to him stood an enormous harrack, greater than any of the others. He was shorter than the elf, but almost three times thicker. He wore a chieftain's helm and bronze glittered among his furs and leathers. Across the shoulders of his chainmail were draped the claws of a bear. He leaned nonchalantly on an immense war-hammer, smug satisfaction etched deep in the stiff fissures of his granite face. Perethor's small voice came shrilly over to them.

'I'm sorry, Curillian.' Was he apologising for betraying them, or for failing them?

It was the harrack chieftain who spoke next, barking with laughter and then grinding out a coarse take on the common speech. It came out like the grating of a portcullis against a gatehouse's stone floor.

'Harrharrharr. So armist king, you pay visit to the city? But, leave so soon?' The harrack was barely capable of inflecting different intonation, but something like sarcasm was conveyed. 'I see you find one my treasures, the elf-witch. But, in haste you not find another...' He beckoned a crony forward, and the Sword of Maristonia sparkled in the torchlight. Almost as tall as the harrack who bore it dutifully forward, it glimmered like a jewel in a coal-heap. Curillian started, rage rising in him.

'That sword is mine, and was my father's, and his father's before him,' he shouted, full of wrath. 'You will give me back my own.'

He reached instinctively to his side to grasp his sword and then remembered that he had none. The harrack's guttural voice came again. The other harracks joined in too, filling the courtyard with a horrible grating noise. Then they stamped their feet in delight. Curillian felt the ground throb between his own feet. Behind him, he felt Carea stir. She crouched down, arms flung forward, and started to incant, but her words were cut off. From out of the ground came stone bonds with vicious speed. Bands of stone, as malleable as any metal, snapped around her ankles; others shot up to seize her wrists, holding them fast, and another encased her head from behind, clamping down over her mouth. Curillian stood aghast, seeing the wild fear in her eyes. She was held fast, unable to do or say anything.

The demonstration of harrack power over elven magic was brutal and overwhelming. Curillian turned his anger on the harrack chieftain.

'Is this how you defeat your enemies? You fear to face them so you encase them in stone? Cowards! Fight me!' He strode forward, eyes blazing his challenge. The lack of response made him shout all the louder. 'Give me a sword, and fight me!'

Still throatily chuckling, the chieftain nodded and beckoned another minion forward. He tossed a sword nonchalantly to Curillian. It clanged dully as it hit the ground and scraped towards him. It was notched all over and as battered as a squire's training post. All the same, Curillian picked it up. He would rather fight with a butcher's cleaver, but it would have to do. Hefting it in his hand, he looked up at the sky, where a few stars peeked through the mists.

Father, I've never needed You more than now. Time and again I've faced death, when all hope was gone, and always You delivered me. Let me win through, let these heathens who curse Your name be delivered into my hands. Give me the strength I need, I have such need of it…

Fortified, he looked down again, sweeping his eyes round the assembled harracks. He sought out one set of eyes after another.

'Who will fight me? Send your best against me!' He looked challengingly at the chieftain. 'If I throw down your champion, you will let us go, myself and the two elves. If I fall, you may take their lives too…'

To his astonishment, the chieftain shrugged, and then nodded.

'As you say, grass-eater. You win, you go free. You lose, you all die. NOW,' he raised his harsh voice. 'SEE MY CHAMPION.'

As if at some hidden signal, the whole place started to shake. The courtyard trembled as if it was in the grip of an earthquake, and masonry flaked away from the surrounding walls. Harracks scattered as something came bursting out of the ground. What Curillian had thought was just a squat statue now turned out to be the head of something much larger. A stone-helmed head rushed upwards, followed by battlemented shoulders and a granite torso. Up and up it rose, straightening legs like mighty arch-posts. The diabolical figure loomed out of a cloud of dust, leaving a mess of rubble and gaping earth. It was ten feet tall, a stone gladiator brought to life. Baleful red eyes looked out in a mockery of true life.

Curillian steadied himself after having been shaken by the thing's emergence. Here was an old legend become reality in front of his eyes. In the Great Wars, seven thousand years and more ago, the elves had fought all the manifold demons of hell's host. If the tales were true, one breed was made of stone but given a monstrous semblance of life in movement and malice, and they had proved unstoppable juggernauts in battle. Carea, had she been able to speak, might have told him more, for it was her kin who had courageously fought against such demons. Not in his worst nightmare did Curillian ever think that he would have to face one. Yet it seemed that one had slept here, beneath the cold floors of Faudunum. Long ago, it must have sought refuge here from the vengeful victors of that ancient conflict. Now it had awoken, rising to meet his challenge.

The demon did not wait long to press its attack, and came stomping towards him like a moving tower. No weapon did it wield or need but its club-like hands, and it came on seeking to trample him like a charging bull. Curillian did the last thing it expected and charged towards it, closing the gap between them even faster. Eyes wide, he slid under the giant arm which came scything round, and as he passed he struck at the demon's thigh with his sword. His momentum took him well past the charging demon, sliding across the flag-stones. He glanced down at his sword. It was snapped off at the hilt. So much for my weapon. He flung it away, knowing he had to reach the Sword of Maristonia somehow. He had never taken it to stone before, but if any blade could harm this monstrosity, then it was the great sword of his forefathers. Forged from a fallen star-shard, blended with unbreakable Zimmerill, the metal of heroes, it was the mightiest weapon ever created. He needed it now.

Slow to realise what its enemy had done, and even slower in lumbering to a halt and turning round, the demon came back for another charge. Curillian saw that his sword was still with the chieftain, who had withdrawn to watch the fight from the safety of a stone platform set in the corner of the courtyard, like a royal viewing box at a tourney. No time to get to it now, he fled before the demon's next onrush, struggling to keep his feet as the earth lurched under the force of the pistoning footfalls. Sprinting for all he was worth, Curillian reached a set of wall-steps and thundered up them. The stone-demon caught up with him and brought a trunk-like arm down, shattering the steps just behind Curillian's heels. *Speed,* thought Curillian, *speed is the key. I must out-manoeuvre him.* He tried to think how the elf-heroes of the ancient days had felled their enemies, or what tactics the fabled Demon-slayers of the dwarves employed, but the thoughts fled before his mind in the panic of staying alive.

Quicker than its lumbering frame would suggest, the demon crashed down its other arm, this time just in front of Curillian, bringing him up sharp. The top of the stairs disintegrated into demolished stone, and he had to fling himself up to reach the parapet. All his pain was drowned in a wave of adrenaline, and he swung himself nimbly up. Suddenly he found himself looking out over the battlements, but only into the next courtyard. He had hoped they were near the outer walls, whence they could escape, but no, they were right in the centre of the fossilised honeycomb of Faudunum. He picked up a dislodged stone, as large as he could manage, and flung it at the unearthly face. It smashed into the stone helmet, and momentarily gave the demon pause, but it did no more damage than a rock-fall to the mountain. The stone-demon returned a stone of his own, one the same size as Curillian. Curillian threw himself flat and gasped as it screeched an inch above his head and crashed into the crenellations. Looking across, Curillian saw a six-foot stretch of battlement blasted clean away.

He catapulted himself to his feet and started to run. He sprinted around the top of the courtyard, following the ramparts, which exploded behind him into smithereens as the stone-demon flailed wildly. No sooner did the demon start to find his range than Curillian quit the wall and hurled himself back down to the courtyard. Crashing into an awkward roll, he came up running like a madman and ducked through the archway that loomed up before him. The harracks were laughing again, enjoying their grim sport. They didn't care where their quarry went, for their pet demon would catch it; nor how much of their city was wrecked in the chase, for it could be rebuilt in no time. Curillian dashed down the corridor he found himself in, hearing it boom and echo with the sound of what was following him. Charging through a hail of falling dust and stone, he hurtled back into the courtyard by another arch, choking and barely able to see. The stone-demon, too big for the corridor, stopped striking the roof and made to give chase in the open again.

Curillian found another set of wall-steps and took to the battlements again. He raced around, making towards the corner where the harracks were watching from their platform. Between him and them, a great bulwark protruded, breaking the run of the rampart with outthrust stone. He saw a long chain hanging down from it and hoped it would reach far enough. Before he could get to it, though, a furious fist struck the stone beneath his feet, trying to pummel right through it. He staggered against the battlements as the rock crumbled under him. Scrambling up again, he ran, hopping and jumping from one embrasure to another. He saw the latest swing of a mighty arm coming, and he leapt right over it, launching himself in a desperate lunge for the chain. He was fully horizontal and just about to plunge down when he caught it, and then he was hurtling through the air on it. He swung, screaming, right around the corner of the bulwark, and just as he sensed the arc come to its limit, he let go and thrust his body forward. Then he was flying through mid-air, borne by the momentum of the swing. He crashed down amongst the harracks feet first with the force of a battering ram. He flattened several of them, and lay stunned and winded.

They were shocked at his sudden appearance in their midst, and were slow to react. Perethor stared at him in abject amazement. In those precious moments, he forced his mutinous body to respond and regained his feet. Shoving violently, he caused further consternation by heaving the harracks nearest to him against their fellows. Picking up a fallen mattock, he lashed out, using the harracks' own weapon against them. He did not intend to fight for long; he just needed to win through to his sword. He focused on the harrack bearing it and battered his way through to him. Evading the swipe of the outraged chieftain, he bulled into the harrack holding his sword and pitched them both from the platform down into the courtyard below. He landed on top of the harrack, breaking his fall at the other's expense. Taking up his sword, he hacked open the harrack's throat and left him spluttering in the dust. Ignoring the tumult above him on the platform, he turned to face the stone-demon.

His opponent had not been idle. With a wrench, it had pulled the chain free from the wall, pulling down half of the tower with it. He was upon Curillian scarce two heartbeats after he had dispatched the harrack. Curillian flung himself backwards in a half-roll, half-somersault to avoid the vast foot that came stomping down to squash him. Coming back up with a war-shout, he attacked the foot while it stood planted. He watched the Sword of Maristonia score along the stone, sparks flying. It did no harm, but it did not break either. It felt good to have it back in his hands, stronger yet lighter than the crude length of iron he'd held before. With it, he felt he had a fighting chance. He struck again, putting all his dwindling strength into the blow. His arms jarred as it connected with the back of the demon's knee, but still it did not bite deep enough. As he withdrew the unbroken blade, its gleam dulled by stone-dust, the demon swung at him as an armist might at an annoying wasp that has just stung him. He was too slow to react, and as he leapt away, the stone fist caught him a glancing blow. He clattered to the floor, head swimming. He just saw the foot coming, and managed to fling himself out of its path in a desperate roll. The demon then tried to pick him up, and Curillian paid it for its folly by shearing off one of its fingers with a flash of his sword. This time the demon reacted, lurching upwards and roaring in pain. *That got him*, Curillian thought.

Taking advantage of the demon's pause, he dashed to where the chain lay torn from its fixings, and took it up. Quick as he could, he flung it round the demon's nearer foot. He was just about to run it around to the other foot when the demon reached down and with surprising dexterity seized the chain. Heaving on it, he sent Curillian flying. Skidding across the ground in a blaze of agony, Curillian forced himself to his feet again as quickly as he could. When the demon let go of the chain, he kept hold of it, dragging it with him on an impulse. He fled the courtyard again, this time by another exit. Larger than the others, it seemed to be a main thoroughfare, which meant the demon was able to follow him. Carrying the chain over one shoulder, and brandishing his sword in the other hand, he darted into a narrow doorway and hurried up the spiralling stairway within, chain clanking behind him. He heard the whump and thump of the demon striking at stone outside, trying to find where he had gone.

Curillian came out on a flat rooftop, and had long enough before the demon spotted him to take his bearings. The flat roof he was on now was joined to another across the street by a narrow bridge, and that rooftop opposite led back to the battlements of the main courtyard.

Dangerously unbalanced by his burdens, he shuffled across the bridge and on to the other rooftop. Now the demon had spotted him and, seeing that it could not reach him from the street below, had found another way up. It battered a whole wall down and used its ruins as a staircase. Meanwhile, Curillian used his bought time well and hurried to where the rooftop backed onto the battlements. He picked a spot between two squat towers and looked out over. To his dismay, there was no rampart beneath him here, only a straight drop of thirty feet down into the courtyard. Hearing the awful noise of his pursuer, he turned and saw the demon scrambling up his makeshift steps. Thinking quickly, he saw iron hooks protruding from the walls of the towers. Hurriedly, he dropped his sword and fastened one end of the chain to one of them. The demon had gained the rooftop now and was rumbling towards him, intent on putting an end to this chase. Curillian felt an odd calm descend on him. He stood, obvious and unafraid in the gap. In his hands, he gripped the length of chain fiercely. Like an avalanche of stone in the mountains, the demon bore down on him, desperate to catch and kill. Either it did not know the courtyard lay so near, or it did not give thought to it. It charged right up to where Curillian waited, and at the last possible second, Curillian dashed to one side, carrying the chain with him.

'MARISTON!' he yelled, fear giving his feet wings. In the blink of an eye, he was gone, and hurled himself against the opposite tower. With all his might, he stretched the chain taut and leaned all his weight against it. The stone-demon had no time to react and clattered into the chain. Its vast weight and momentum carried it forward until it tripped and fell headlong into the courtyard. The whole city shook and dust rose in plumes as the great gladiator crashed down in ruin.

In the eerie silence that followed, Curillian retrieved his precious sword. He cast down the chain and lowered himself wearily down into the maelstrom of stone and dust. Picking his way forward, he walked past the stone helmet, which lay quite still. From their high platform, the harracks were looking down, appalled. Curillian staggered out into full view of them, and looked up. For a long moment there was silence, except for the sound of small bits of stone pattering down. Curillian heard the stirring behind him even as he saw the expression on the harrack chieftain's face change from one of shocked horror to smug triumph. He turned to face his enemy, knowing he had no strength to fight again. The stone-demon was trying to rise, prying itself up from the indent it had made in the floor of the courtyard.

Then, something else happened. Snaking tendrils of vegetation suddenly appeared, emerging out of cracks in the ground. Vines and tree-roots, thin at first, but then waxing thicker, crawled all over the demon, festooning it like overgrown ruins. The weight of them tugged it back down to the floor. More and more came, and tighter they tugged on the scarred stone. Curillian turned his head, and through clouds of dust, saw Carea, still bound fast but with one hand free. The fall of the demon must have broken one of her bonds. With her one hand, she wove the spell, controlling the vegetation. Slowly the roots exerted intense pressure, and Curillian saw them bunching like muscles. He watched as all the age-long grip of trees condensed down into the fury of a few seconds. A deep groaning sound arose and grew louder and louder until suddenly an almighty crack rent the air. A dozen other cracks followed and then all was still. Slithering away as quickly as they had come, the vines and tree-roots vanished, leaving the stone-demon splintered into a dozen different pieces.

Turning back to Carea, he watched her other bonds fall away, as if they had been held in place by the life of the stone-demon. She was weak, though, and with the spell now done, she collapsed back to the floor, spent. Curillian went to her and cradled her in his arms. He feared the awesome output had killed her already frail life-force. She smiled wanly up at him. Weariness overcame him as he knelt there with her. He heard the tramping of boots as the harracks stomped down from their platform and surrounded them in a wide circle. Crossbows were shouldered and aimed at the pathetic pair of figures in the courtyard's centre. Looking from Carea to the poised harracks, Curillian blinked away tears. His end had come. Grasping his sword to him, and still hugging Carea tight, he turned his mind to Prélan. His prayer muffled the sound of the crossbow bolts being loosed, but when they burst into flame in mid-air, his mind snapped back to reality. The war cry seemed to come from all sides at once.

'MARISTON!'

IV

Into the Black

AGAINST All hope, they made it to the foot of the walls without being spotted. Evening was fast falling into night. Skirting round the outer ramparts, they had come to the back of the eerie fortress and crouched now in the shelter of a few sparse pine trees. The armists paused, trying to get their breath back, but Sin-Serin looked fearful and anxious to press on. Did she sense something the rest of them did not? The obstacle of the wall daunted them all, for there seemed to be no way up it. They had ropes with them, but no grapnel-hooks to latch onto the battlements. They had taken great pains to avoid the guarded main gate, but now they had come to an insurmountable barrier. No postern gates or sally ports were there, just sheer stone. Sin-Serin looked around, surveying the terrain immediately around them.

'Cut down one of the trees,' she commanded. They looked at her as if she were mad, but Roujeark saw that even saying the words pained the wood-elf.

'What are you thinking, elf?' Lancoir challenged her. 'We've got no time to play at lumber-jacks!'

'I will get us in, but I need a tree.'

Roujeark looked up and saw that the trees, although poor stunted specimens, were nearly as tall as the wall. Did Sin-Serin think she could make a ramp by leaning one of the trees against the wall? Lancoir looked as if he were about to object again, but then he gave the nod to the other armists. Aleinus, Antaya and Findor took out their axes. Lancoir and Roujeark joined them and together they hacked at the nearest pine. Fearful of the chopping noises giving them away, they bent to the work with feverish haste. With a crack and a drawn-out groan, the tree surrendered its uprightness and toppled over. Roujeark was dismayed by the noise it made, and even more so to see it fall short of the wall – maybe it wouldn't reach after all? But Sin-Serin was not perturbed. Under her direction, she had them strip away all the smaller branches, leaving just the long, thin trunk.

'Now pick it up,' the elf ordered. The armists hesitated again, but they complied when they saw the determined confidence in her face. Heaving, the five armists lifted the fallen trunk and held it waist-high. Sin-Serin looped one coil of rope over her shoulder and took up the front of the trunk. She looked up at the wall, sizing it up.

'Back up,' she hissed, and they shuffled awkwardly backwards. Speaking softly, the elf gave them last instructions over her shoulder. 'When I give the word, run for all you're worth toward the wall. When you can't run any further, keep holding the trunk and push it upwards. I'll do the rest.' The armists exchanged bewildered looks with each other, none of them understanding. They weren't given time for further reflection.

'Now!' hissed Sin-Serin.

They started forward and soon broke into a lumbering trot. They built up all the speed they could thus encumbered and charged towards the wall. When Sin-Serin reached the foot of the wall, she flung her legs upward, planting them on the wall. Keeping a hold of the trunk, she walked quickly upwards. Aleinus was the next to reach the wall, and he came up short. Staggering under the weight, he nevertheless managed to angle the trunk upwards, levering Sin-Serin higher. One by one they all came to a halt and then switched their efforts to lifting the trunk. Intuitive understanding came to them as they watched Sin-Serin propelled higher, and they strained upwards. Lancoir was at the back with the heaviest section of the trunk, and he thrust upward with the force of two armists. Hand over hand they passed the trunk upward, ignoring splinters, and the higher it went the more they struggled to keep it steady. Had Sin-Serin not been guiding it from the top, it would have fallen. Eventually they ran out of trunk and gave one last heave. Sin-Serin was nearly at the top. Their last upward shove unbalanced them and they lost control of the trunk. With no support beneath it anymore, the trunk swayed to one side as if in a re-enactment of its original felling moments before. Sin-Serin, though, was equal to the challenge, and even as the trunk lurched sideways, she let go of it and stretched upward for handholds. Another few inches and she would have been out of reach of tiny skirting-shelf of rock just below the battlements. The trunk crashed down sideways, deflecting off the wall and rolling down the slope.

Sin-Serin was left hanging by her fingertips, agonisingly short of the battlements. Had it all been for nothing? Roujeark thought. But no, as they watched, craning their necks upwards, she shifted her grip and turned herself so she was no longer facing the wall but outwards. They had no idea how she managed to maintain her grip in that position, but she did so, fingers straining. Momentarily she looked as helpless as a criminal chained to a wall, but then she rocked her legs outwards. Again and again, she swung her legs, building momentum, and then, just as she lost her grip, she surged upwards in an acrobatic summersault. Defying gravity, she let go of the wall and soared heels over head in a backward arc. Their hearts were in their mouths as they watched her, but she landed on the embrasure between two flanks of parapet with all the poise and finesse of a professional tumbler. Not wasting a second, she sprang lightly down out of sight. She disappeared for such a long time that they began to grow disconcerted, but then they heard a muffled thump. Moments later, she reappeared and cast the rope down to them. She had made its end fast to the battlement so they would be able to climb up. One by one, they shinned up the rope, thankful that they had had an easier time of it than their guide.

'That was a neat trick,' Lancoir told her grudgingly as he dropped over onto the rampart's walkway. Roujeark was astonished to see unshed tears shining in the elf's eyes as she answered.

'The pine may only have been a poor stunted creature, living in shadow, but it gave its life for us.' Lancoir nodded, acknowledging the sentiment for no more than a split second. Then he was up.

'Time is short, we must go.' They passed the slumped figure of the harrack sentry that Sin-Serin had dispatched, but they did not see any others.

'Where are they all?'

'Something is happening in this city,' Sin-Serin responded, as if she could sense it through the stones. 'A distraction is benefitting us, and there's only one cause I can think of.'

'The king,' said Lancoir grimly. He redoubled their pace. Suddenly their progress round the outer rampart was brought up short by a great tremor, which ran all through the city and shook the stone beneath their feet. Sin-Serin spoke urgently to them, fear in her normally serene eyes.

'A great evil is stirring, we must hurry.'

'How do we know where to find the king?' asked Caréysin.

'Follow the noise,' the elf told him, rushing past. True enough, there followed an ominous series of sounds, thumps and crashes, all of it portending destruction. Roujeark even saw a cloud of dust rising in the night air ahead of them, out of the heart of the city, and he wondered fearfully what was going on.

They saw other harracks as they went but none of them paid any heed, or even showed any sign that they had seen the intruders at all. The armist party had kept to the rooftops and upper ways, but down below, at street level, harracks were hurrying towards the centre of the city in their scores. Unmistakably, something had them so concerned that they were heedless of all else. Roujeark could understand their preoccupation: the tumult sounded as if the city was being torn apart. What was going on? Up ahead, torchlight peeped garishly out from a great open space, the only light in the whole cold citadel. It was partially obscured by clouds of dust, but it gave them something to aim for.

After an infuriating series of wrong turns, they finally found a way to reach the torchlight. A crooked stair brought them up a squat tower, which overlooked a great courtyard. Through the roiling dust, they saw first a ring of harracks with crossbows, and then a forlorn pair of figures huddling together in the middle. Heaps of stones and fallen masonry lay everywhere, and Sin-Serin, normally so taciturn, gasped when she saw the broken stones still resembling the outline of an enormous stone figure.

The armists crouched helplessly, even Lancoir unsure of what to do, but Roujeark's mind was suddenly sharp and incisive. Even before he had taken in all the details of the scene below, he knew that the king was the figure in the middle of the harracks, and he knew also that their crossbows were about to fire. Feeling a throb of power bursting to life within him, he stretched out his arms, and the wildfire surged down them. The crossbow bolts were loosed with ragged, mechanical coughs. Simultaneously his fingertips ignited into flame, and, quicker than thought, that flame spread to the bolts in mid-air. No trail of fire connected his glowing hands with the bolts – this time he had managed to ignite the flames where he wanted them. The bolts never reached their targets – so hot did the flames burn that they were consumed in an instant and fell in showers of ash to the courtyard floor.

Lancoir was shaken out of his uncertainty by the spectacle of Roujeark's power. It was the turn of him and his guards now. He bellowed a war cry that was soon taken up and repeated by his companions.

'MARISTON!'

With ropes tied to the tower's battlements, Lancoir and the six guardsmen flung themselves over the edge and abseiled rapidly down into the courtyard. Caréysin fired a quick succession of arrows at the harracks and then followed the others. Once they hit the floor, they charged towards their beleaguered king. The suddenness of their appearance gave them the edge of a few crucial seconds. The bewildered harrack crossbowmen had barely recovered from the shock of their vaporised bolts when the armists were on them. Swords crashed down onto the crossbows, splintering them, but the harracks themselves were harder to destroy. The heaviest blows managed to bite into them, but anything less than a full-blooded chop seemed to jump back, thwarted. It did not take them long to begin fighting back, nor for more harracks to lumber into the fray, brandishing their mattocks. There followed a desperate skirmish in the courtyard, garishly illuminated by the flames.

Lancoir made straight for the king. The moment the crossbow bolts had burst into flame Curillian had leapt to his feet, brandishing his great sword in defence of the elf slumped beside him. Lancoir knew better than to underestimate his king, but all the same, he looked bone-weary, just about ready to collapse. He dared not think what he had already been through. So, he rushed to his side and stood back to back with him. Several harracks drew near, menacing brutes in the firelight.

'Lancoir,' Curillian called over his shoulder. 'We must get out of here. We'll be surrounded soon.' Lancoir glanced back at his king.

'We'll have to fight our way out. Can you manage it?' The king's look was savage.

'I'll die before this sword leaves my hands again.' As if to prove his point, he lashed out and hewed a harrack's head clean from his shoulders. The Sword of Maristonia had no trouble cleaving the thick, leathery skin that was turning other blades.

The armists were hard-pressed to defend themselves when the harracks came up in force. Killing them was hard enough, but until the killing blow was dealt, they seemed to feel no pain at all. All the remaining Royal Guards were thrown back and staring death in the face when Lionenn came to their rescue. Wielding his stolen mattock, he came charging through the harracks like a maddened bull. Sweeping his weapon left and right, he bludgeoned several harracks and stamped them into the ground. His victory was brief, though, for a heavy mattock blow from behind knocked him down, club clattering on the courtyard floor. The harracks pressed in close again and the armists were hemmed in with their king and captain. Sin-Serin was nowhere to be seen, although visibility in the courtyard was poor.

Lancoir was just readying himself for a hopeless last stand when the harrack in front of him burst into flames. His thick furs caught fire like a pitch-soaked torch. Then the same thing happened to another, and then another. Just then, Roujeark came striding through the ruddy dust-clouds like an avenging angel. Utterly different from how they had seen him before, he looked like an armist possessed. He was now wielding his fire with full confidence, and at his coming, a whole ring of the harracks had been ignited. Panic-stricken, they dropped their weapons and went into a mad, whirling dance. They rent the air with unearthly shrieks and caused mayhem among those of their own kind who were not yet on fire.

'NOW,' shouted Lancoir, 'RUN FOR IT!'

Curillian paused only long enough to sling Carea across his shoulder, and then they were all moving. The harracks had fled before them, and Roujeark and Findor followed as a rear-guard. They stumbled blindly forward, tripping over fallen masonry, and then met Sin-Serin coming back through the dust. She beckoned them forward, seemingly knowing the way. She led them to a small archway where a pathetic figure was huddled. Curillian saw that it was Perethor, cringing and sobbing.

'He comes with us,' he told Lancoir. No sooner had he said the words than an enormous figure leapt down at them from above. Curillian and Lancoir were knocked flat in opposite directions, but Curillian was the first up, sword ready. It was the harrack chieftain, whom he had not seen since he had won back his sword. A mad angry light was in the chieftain's eyes, and he came at his erstwhile prisoner with a mace studded with metal barbs. Curillian backed away from the savage onset, evading the massive swings of the mace. Then he stepped smartly to one side and cut down, cleaving the chieftain's mace-hand off at the wrist. Weaponless, the enormous harrack still tried to rush him, seeking to crush him against the wall with his sheer weight, but again Curillian gave way before him. He bought himself enough space and then crouched low. Putting all his strength into a great sideways swing, he cut the harrack's legs out from under him. The chieftain went down heavily, screaming like a wounded boar. Curillian glanced at the hateful face, twisted in a paroxysm of pain and rage, only for a moment before ending his enemy's life with a sword-tip through his neck.

The fight had only lasted thirty seconds, but it had given the other harracks a chance to regroup. Curillian pointed his sword at Perethor, and said again, 'He comes with us.'

'Yes,' agreed Sin-Serin, 'my kinsman here will show us the way out.' The wood-elf looked at Carea, eyes full of concern, as her unconscious kinself lay slumped over the king's broad shoulder. But when she returned her attention to Perethor, the snow-elf hurriedly pulled himself together and led them through the arch-way. He nearly died a moment later when a harrack swung a mattock at him from round a corner, but the brutal blow missed by a hair's breadth and struck the wall, sending shards of stonework flying. Lancoir slew him with a mighty thrust and, pushing him aside, cleared the path. More harracks had returned to harry them from the rear, but Findor kept them at bay until Roujeark put the fear of fire into them again. Then they were on the move, fleeing through the cold passageways of Faudunum, dodging the slingshots and crossbow bolts loosed at them. Along chill tunnels and through cheerless streets they ran, all weariness forgotten in their desperation to escape. Perethor led them unerringly through many twists and turns, though barely a landmark did they pass. Several times they were accosted, but Lancoir seemed invincible as he cut down all who stood in his path.

Perethor led them round one last corner and suddenly they came to a downward slope that led to the outer walls thirty yards away. But he stopped abruptly, brought up short by what unexpectedly lay before him. The harracks had opened up a gutter in the street and filled it with an oily substance. No sooner had the escapers emerged round the corner than they set torches to the oil and instantaneously, a wall of fire scorched before them. Roujeark was not the only one who had fire at his disposal, it seemed. Through the searing heat, they could glimpse a gatehouse on the other side, their way of escape now beyond reach.

Perethor did not tarry long, leading them instead down another street. Running round a few more corners, he led them into an open space that was dominated by a hillock of rock. In the rock-face an arch was set, beyond which all was dark. Perethor plunged through the arch and into the blackness beyond. The armists hesitated only for a moment before following. Inside, all was pitch black until Perethor struck up a torch. Its fiery light revealed a well-hewn tunnel that sloped down before them, twisting away into the bowels of the city. Down the slope they ran, following its spiralling course deeper and deeper. Over the sound of their feet, they could hear the pursuit close behind, following them down underground. Where was this strange elf leading them?

At the bottom of the slope, they came to a smaller opening, a narrow gallery running into the rock at a slight downward angle and supported by wooden posts. A warm wind wafted up to them out of the depths. At the entrance to the shaft was a bulky dram made of cast iron. The huge dirty conveyance had four under-sized wheels, which rested on crude iron tracks on the shaft's floor. When Perethor told them to get in, the armist guards looked at him as if he were crazy, but he insisted.

'There's only one other way out of this mine, and its way down there,' he pointed down the shaft. 'It's either back up the tunnel to where the harracks are hunting for us, or further down, and it'll be faster by dram.'

Curillian led by example. He laid Carea in the dram and climbed in after her. Hurriedly the rest piled in, squeezing themselves into the narrow space. Perethor jumped in last, and as he did so, he released a huge iron lever beside them. With a grating sound, the dram seemed to come alive, and started to inch down the slope. The armists were alarmed to be moving, but Perethor was quite calm, and stayed holding another lever like a helmsman at a ship's tiller.

Their nerves grew as the dram quickly picked up speed, rolling on its tracks down into the darkness. Lancoir crouched at the front, holding the torch aloft as their only light and staring wide-eyed down the tunnel as it sped by quicker and quicker. Suddenly a gust of warm wind extinguished the torch and they were plunged into darkness. Screams were stifled, but panic-stricken terror surged up within all of them as the wobbling dram hurtled down into the darkness. They were sloshed around like slops in a bucket as the dram rounded corners, and their stomachs leapt into their mouths when they plunged down sudden drops. Above the whistling of the wind, Perethor's voice came to them out of the darkness.

'Stay calm, we'll slow down soon. We're coming to the habitable parts. There's light there.' True enough, they entered onto a long slow incline and they decelerated gradually until they were just rolling at walking pace. The darkness lifted somewhat as a ruddy light waxed stronger ahead and above them. Perethor insisted they all lie flat and be silent, so it was only by peeping over the edge that Lancoir saw their destination. They rolled slowly into what looked like a docking station, wooden boardwalks built on either side of the tracks, which now reached their terminus. Wall-braziers flickered, and in their light he could see a pair of harracks guarding the station. They seemed surprised by the unannounced arrival, and got slowly to their feet to inspect. As they approached, Lancoir gestured to his companions, and swords were readied. The two harracks leaned over the dram to look in from opposite sides, and the reward of their curiosity was a blade in the gullet. Their blood poured down, drenching the huddled fugitives, but they never had a chance to make a sound above a fleshy gurgling.

Disgusted, Roujeark couldn't get out of the dram fast enough. They all scrambled out, but Perethor went ahead, stealing quietly up the boardwalk to check their situation. While he was gone, the rest waited around anxiously, straining their ears for sounds of pursuit. Was there another dram to bring harracks after them? What lay ahead? Carea was barely conscious, leaning against Curillian, but they heard her say one intelligible word.

'Cloaks…their cloaks…' With a vague arm gesture, she pointed at the dead harracks. Lancoir quickly took her meaning.

'A disguise. Quick, take their cloaks, their helmets too.' He and Curillian fastened the thick bearskin cloaks over the top of their own clothes, wrinkling their noses at the smell, and placed the ugly iron caps on their heads. More apparel of the same sort was hanging from hooks beside the boardwalk, as if the station were meant to have more guards but was under-manned. Very soon, all of them were transformed into passable harracks. By that time, Perethor had returned from his reconnaissance.

'The coast is clear…for now. Come, we must be quick.'

When the boardwalk ended, the tunnel broadened and the ceiling opened out above them into a cavern. The light of wall-torches grew stronger and side passages started to appear. They soon saw that what they had taken for a mine was really an underground settlement, and quite an extensive one at that. They realised that there was more of Faudunum below ground than there was above. The chinking of hammers was all around, and the grinding of wheels and the echoing of distant feet and voices. They drew their stolen cloaks about them, and looking around they spotted harracks here and there. Some gave them suspicious looks, but none accosted them, and they hurried on. There were workshops and forges, sleeping areas, halls full of tables, benches, and kitchens, which smelt of red meat and strong ale.

Just as more attention was starting to be paid to them, they left the open caverns behind and passed into another tunnel. They were astonished to find a team of mules harnessed to a big waggon, full of barrels and boxes. It seemed to be some sort of supply vehicle. The mules were grazing from troughs of hay built into the walls, seemingly unattended. Fearing discovery at any minute, Perethor ushered them up into the waggon. As hurriedly as they could, they stowed themselves uncomfortably amid the cargo, while Perethor and Lancoir took up seats on the driver's bench. Just as a couple of harracks appeared in the tunnel behind them, they cracked the whips and rumbled off. The waggon's rickety wooden wheels bounced and trundled over snags and divots on the tunnel floor. The creaking of the waggon and the clip-clop of the mules' hooves seemed loud in their ears, but no trouble came.

After a while, though, they rounded a bend and saw a crossroad ahead. Wooden barricades and sentries guarded the underground junction. Involuntarily they pulled on the reins and slowed down, pulling their hoods down over their heads. They were spotted, and there was nowhere they could go except back up the tunnel. Lancoir hoped they could somehow bluff their way through. Was Perethor known down here and able to come and go? One of the sentries stepped into their path and the mules stopped of their own accord. The guard barked a word. Lancoir looked sidelong out of his hood at Perethor, but the elf beside him gave no sign. The order was repeated, more fiercely, but still Lancoir did not answer, but just sat hunched on the bench. He could feel the tension among his comrades in the bed of the waggon behind him. Impatient and suspicious now, the guard walked right alongside Lancoir and looked up at him, hefting a spear. Slowly, almost delicately, the harrack used his spear-point to push Lancoir's hood back. For a lingering second there was a startled silence, and something like bewilderment showed in the guard's face. Lancoir smiled at him, and booted him full in the mouth. Stunned, the guard fell back, and as he did so, Lancoir seized his spear. Beside him, Perethor cracked on the reins, geeing the mules on. Lurching forward, they burst through the wooden barricade, accompanied by the angry shouts of the other guards. Lancoir righted the spear and hurled it at one of the harracks as they careered past, pinning him against the wall of the tunnel.

Suddenly they were clear of the crossroads, plunging down the tunnel on the opposite side. The passageways behind them were alive with hoarse shouting now, a din that echoed menacingly down the confined space to them. They thundered on at breakneck pace. In one place, they passed a more open stretch where harracks crossbowmen stalked on a gallery above them. Bolts were loosed, but in a few seconds they had passed safely back into an enclosed tunnel. One quarrel had pierced a barrel of ale, and as they went, it spewed a frothy trail behind them. Aleinus cupped his hands together and slurped down a handful, breaking out into something between a grin and a grimace.

'Bleugh, it's not good stuff, but if I'm going to die, I'd rather have a drink in me!' Little did he or the others realise, though, that another bolt had hobbled one of the mules, and already they were slowing. Lancoir cracked the reins, but then they slewed and struck a protruding rock. It snapped off the back-left wheel, and the whole waggon lurched down to one side. The pierced barrel of ale teetered off and smashed on the floor, its frothing contents washing down the tunnel. They could go no further in the waggon, so they extricated themselves from the wreck, and prepared to go on by foot. But just then, they heard voices, and saw torchlight flickering up out of a side-tunnel. Lancoir looked down and saw a detachment of harrack soldiers storming up some stairs towards them. He knew swords wouldn't last long, so he called for the only missile to hand.

'Antaya, Andil, roll me one of those barrels.'

The two guards retrieved one of the casks, and rolled it along to their captain. In a show of tremendous strength, Lancoir lifted it up on high, just as a crowd of harracks emerged round a bend of the stairs into plain view. Lancoir hurled the barrel at them. It smashed into them and the wood burst asunder. Wood and ale exploded outwards in a foaming explosion, and the lead harracks were knocked back down the stairs, taking those behind with them. With the raucous din of their dismay ringing in their ears, the company carried on their way, hurrying as quickly as their tired limbs would allow. Perethor's call was a welcome relief when his words sank in.

'Not far to the gate now, keep going!'

They did, following the crooked tunnel ever downwards. Before long, they could see a brighter light ahead than the occasional wall-sconces. It came from a large space at the tunnel's bottom, where it expired in a great underground porch. Large pillars hewn into the hillside marked a smooth section of the rock-face. Two harracks were manning the gate, and they were ready for them, having heard them coming. Lancoir hacked down one, but the other nearly accounted for Curillian. Encumbered by Carea, Curillian just managed to avoid an axe-swing before Andil came to his aid and chopped off the harrack's arm, axe and all. In a few moments both gate-guards lay dead, but then the fugitives were brought up short. The gate appeared to be no gate at all, just a wall of stone where a gate should have been. It seemed the harracks didn't use wood for anything if they could use stone.

'How do we get out?' cried Aleinus, angry and frustrated. Wordlessly Perethor darted into an enclosed space to one side of the gate. Moments later, they heard a grinding noise as some hidden mechanism kicked into life. Before their eyes, the whole wall started inching upwards like a solid-stone portcullis. Throwing himself flat, Aleinus shouted that this was indeed the way out; he could see the world outside, but it was twenty feet away with solid stone hanging over the exit. To make matters worse, the gate was infuriatingly slow, only creeping upwards.

'Better get it to hurry up,' called Findor, who had gone back to the tunnel mouth to watch. 'They're coming!'

Sure enough, they could all hear the rumbling of many booted feet bearing down on them. Sin-Serin dropped flat as soon as there was enough space, and rolled herself through the aperture. Lancoir watched her do it, and shouted for the others to do likewise.

'Follow the bloody elf!' he roared, pushing Aleinus flat again and practically kicking him through the opening. He beckoned for Roujeark to do likewise. Curillian had rolled Carea under, where Sin-Serin took her up, and then followed himself. The gate was now waist-high. Antaya helped the groggy Lionenn down and then ducked through himself.

Just then, the harrack pursuers appeared. Dozens of them came pounding out of the tunnel like a rock-fall, and with barely a check in pace, they charged at the gate. Lancoir and Findor stood as a rear-guard, ready to do battle. Lancoir's blood was up, and he booted the first harrack back before cutting into him with a sideways swing of his sword. Findor accounted for another, before Lancoir blazed at him to get gone. Perethor reappeared a moment later, dragged from the guardroom by some harracks. In the confusion, he managed to snatch himself away and dive for the growing aperture. Lancoir cut down the harrack who lunged after him, flattening him with a vicious downward chop of his sword. Then he himself dove for the gap, rolling into the space and out into the world beyond. He was up and running in the blink of an eye, but Perethor stumbled and fell. The harracks, who came pouring out of the gate in pursuit, were on him in a moment, but Lancoir changed direction hastily and bulled into them. Hacking all about him, he bought enough time for Perethor to get away before wrenching himself free and retreating himself.

The terrain outside the gate was a rough downward slope, set well down the hill from the citadel on the summit. Not far ahead of them, though, the isolated Hill of Faudunum ran into the steep slopes of the valley beyond, which led back up into the mountains. A narrow, dipping saddle of land joined the hill to the mountain slopes beyond, and the whole area was covered with small, stalwart fir trees. The escapers fled down to the saddle, thinking to take refuge in the trees, but the harracks followed them, bent on revenge. Sin-Serin, still carrying Carea, led them on up the far slope, but they did not have the strength to go far.

Roujeark's energy was giving out, drained by the power that had burst out of him. Was it the fire within him subsiding, or was the air suddenly getting colder? They were running into a fine mist that seemed to be thickening with every step. Finally, they could go no further. As one, they turned to face their attackers, resolved on a final stand. The harracks themselves were toiling on the slope, squat figures on short legs, but when they saw their enemy at bay, they put on an extra spurt. The armists brandished their swords, and Sin-Serin and Caréysin bent their bows, as two-score harracks charged closer. But even as the escapers looked on-coming death in the face, strange war cries suddenly rent the cold night air. Wild ululating voices filled the misty air like fell beasts issuing forth. Then, the air around them became alive with angry objects whizzing by. Buzzing past their ears like maddened wasps, the missiles came from behind them and smacked into the oncoming harracks. Roujeark looked behind him, but in the mist, he could only see vague shadowy forms darting here and there. More missiles came, missing them, but striking down the harracks. With unerring accuracy, they struck the harracks in their eyes, felling them instantly with horrible squishing noises. The harracks thumped to the ground in droves.

Roujeark looked back again, and this time saw ghostly white figures running down-slope, swinging slingshots and screeching strange war cries. It was the Cuherai, the snow-elves, come to their rescue. They came through the trees like frozen banshees, and the missiles they hurled were lethal little pellets of ice. Little more than irritating when they struck armour or thick clothing, they were deadly against vulnerable parts. The snow-elves knew to go for the eyes of their tough-skinned enemies, and their accuracy was appalling.

Half the harracks were dead already. The snow-elves surged past the fugitives' defensive line and on down the slope. As they went, the very breath of their mouths seemed to freeze the air around them so that the world became like the inside of a winter cloud. The tendrils of freezing vapour dampened sound and visibility. As though from a great distance, they heard muffled groans and gasps as the remaining harracks either turned and fled back to their gate or were frozen solid were they stood.

Just as soon as the snow-elves came, they departed again. While their out-runners were dealing with the harracks, others came and hurried the escapers away. There were not many of them, but they seemed to be everywhere at once. Swiftly they retreated back up the slope, urging their friends up with them. When the exhausted armists could go no further, they collapsed. Silent sledges were brought up, and the fugitives were placed on them. In a trice they were on the move again, vanishing uphill at breath-taking speed. They did not stop for a long time, not until Faudunum was left far behind, and by that time the night air had cleared. They were in the Black Mountains again. Most of the guards lay asleep, and Carea and Curillian, side by side, seemed overcome with weariness. Even Lancoir had submitted himself to the necessity of riding on a sledge, and now sat nodding, countless wounds left untended.

Roujeark, although bone-tired, found himself prickled by a strange wakefulness. He saw now that the sledges' sinewy hide ropes had been whisked upwards by packs of white wolves, slim but exceedingly fleet of foot. Now they sat around in a pack, panting and steaming. While the beasts were resting, the snow-elf leader came up, Aiiyosha herself. She made straight for where Perethor stood apprehensively among the armists. Several snow-elves stood nearby, like guards. The chieftain stalked right up to Perethor, stopping inches from his face. No words were spoken, but her fierce gaze made the rescued elf quail. Upon some hidden understanding, Perethor cringed and began to whimper pitifully, even as both arms seized him. Startled, Roujeark stumbled after as Perethor was dragged away into the night. The rest of the armists were oblivious as he was led away to the edge of a precipice. Fearing what was about to happen, Roujeark tried to intervene, but a snow-elf shoved him away. He came on again, but this time he was brought up short by the ice-blade suddenly held under his chin. All he could do was watch as Perethor was forced to his knees. Standing behind him, grasping him by the hair, Aiiyosha produced an ice-blade, pale and wickedly sharp. Looking up to heaven, as if in sacrificial ceremony, she uttered baleful words and drew the dagger redly across her victim's throat. While Perethor's life-blood was still gushing forth, he was picked up and hurled bodily into the depths.

V

Potent Persuasion

'HE Was a wanted elf,' Curillian told Roujeark. They were sitting together on a mossy stone. The shock of what he had witnessed still trembled in Roujeark. 'I thought he had just gone missing near Faudunum,' the king continued, 'but truth is that Perethor was an exile. He entered into it willingly, to escape the penalty for his crime.'

'What crime?' Roujeark asked.

'He raped a kinself. Fleeing to Faudunum was his only way of escape. It was a desperate measure, for there is little love between snow and stone. There he became a traitor, buying his life with secrets harmful to his kin. Wretched soul that he was, he soon yearned to return to his kin; yet he had no means of escape, nor any certainty that he would be received back with forgiveness. Maybe he hoped to expiate his sin by rescuing the princess, but he dared not attempt it until I came along. In the end, he helped, and I couldn't have done it without him, but he burned his bridges with the harracks. The traitor betrayed his masters, but he must have known he was going back to his death. Now I have lived to see the ruthlessness of Cuherai justice.'

The king fell silent, contemplating the right and wrong of it. In the end, he laid the matter aside, and, rising, he went to say farewell to his host. All his company was ready, refreshed and waiting for him. For a week, they had been succoured by their rescuers, strengthened by their broths and kept warm by their curious shelters. Now they were ready to set forth, and Curillian thanked Aiiyosha for all her kindness. The enigmatic snow-elf smiled and uttered over her guest a blessing after the fashion of her own kind. Carea and Sin-Serin said their own farewell, the wood speaking to the snow, kindred yet alien.

The snow-elves vanished almost before their very eyes, leaving them alone in the wilderness. Thick clouds were about them, obscuring the vistas on either side. Curillian took counsel with Sin-Serin and Carea, who had spent long hours in silent companionship with each other.

'Where are we to go next? Back to the forest?' he asked them. The princess was much stronger now, thanks to her time with the snow-elves, but her ordeal still lay heavily on her shoulders. She was frail and hunched, grey of face and withdrawn. Not a word had she spoken since their escape until now.

'No,' she said. 'Not to the forest. Your path lies ahead of you and not back. Sin-Serin, take us along the mountains' feet to Eldaphir's spring.'

'To Eldaphir I will go,' agreed Sin-Serin. 'It is the longer road home, but the fairer, and the safer.'

So their journey began again. Leaving that cold high place, they struck northward, leaving the perilous vale of Stonad behind them. Sin-Serin led them, and for a time their going was slow as they kept to the pace of Carea. She was silent, completely withdrawn into herself, and though she stumbled often and tired quickly, she kept going. Curillian watched her with worried eyes, but gradually he saw the colour coming back into her cheeks, if not the shadow lifting from her soul. Their going was slow also because of the terrain, which was difficult and tangled. Through deep ravines and over rock-strewn moors they trudged, winding ever northward through the tangled foothills. Every once in a while the persistent clouds would lift to reveal tantalising glimpses of glistening peaks above them, but to their right, the lower slopes seemed trapped under an impenetrable blanket of grey.

𝄃

One night Curillian felt himself wakened by a strange sensation, like the caress of a passing mist. Looking up, he saw the outline of Carea stooped over him. It was still night, and he feared that something was wrong. But she put a finger to her lips, and bade him follow her. As he stumbled through the darkness, Curillian noticed that the stars were visible for the first time in many a night, and his breath misted in front of him. Unerringly Carea led him out of their little camp and into the darkness. She made for a pinnacle of rock rearing out from the dark hillside and started to climb. Up and up they went, the rock slope becoming steeper and steeper until they were climbing almost vertically. Her energy has certainly returned, thought Curillian. She was not satisfied until they had climbed right to the top, and inched along a narrow finger of rock, which overhung the hillside beneath. She sat them down, facing east, and Curillian saw the first hint of dawn tinging the horizon. Nothing obstructed his view to the east: all of Kalimar lay before them, shrouded in sleepy mists.

Giving no word of explanation, Carea just sat beside him in silence. There was no wind, all was still. Together they watched the world come slowly alive. Time as slow as the unfolding of the world passed as the light blue ribbon waxed larger, reaching into the sky until it was a broad swathe. Behind it came the vermillion band of nascent sunlight, creeping above the rim of the world and flushing into a thousand shades as it did so. Behind its fiery out-runners, the brilliance of the sun's onset lit up the sky, and suddenly the land below them began to be revealed. Curillian gave an involuntary gasp as the first slither of the sun's disc peeped above the horizon. Shy at first, then bolder and brighter, the sun rose until the whole elven kingdom was awash with golden splendour.

'I feel re-born,' Carea told him. He turned to look at her, and saw her face suffused with life. 'I have waited for just such a morning as this, a sign that all will be well. I have been lost in dark dreams...'

Curillian felt himself drawn in by her words and lost in the dream world they conjured about him. The great elven minstrels and storytellers could bring waking visions to life before their audience's eyes with the power of their words, and scarcely less potent was Carea's voice in that hour. Soon he ceased to hear them at all, but seemed to know them in his own mind. Vividly she retold the story of her capture, of how she had come to rescue a friend who had become ensnared in Faudunum, only to become caught herself.

Many allies strove with her to uncover the plots of the mountain-dwellers, but this one had probed too deeply, and needed rescue. Dread of the harracks and their rock-magic had not held Carea back, for she was of the royal line of Firnar, and great in power. Truly, had her mind not been focused on rescuing the captive, her power could have overthrown the city of the harracks, but the trap had been well laid. Keeping her within sight, the harracks had taken the captive ahead of her, leading her deeper and deeper into the earth. Wrathful, Carea's radiance in that dark place had been like a star fallen into a mine, but too little did she heed her surroundings. She took on the form of a sparrow to penetrate in through the narrow opening of the prison and, once within, was too late in changing back to prevent the slaying of the captive. Only then did she mark the form of the prison, an impervious square of delved rock with but one opening.

That opening was now shut behind her, airtight and sealed with many locks. They had lured her into a tomb beyond the reach of any.

All of her magic could not avail her in that place, shut off in a lightless void. Bereft of the sunlight, wind, and wood that she thrived upon, she slowly faded in that place. As her vitality ebbed away, she came to understand all too well the efficacy of rock-magic in its own environment. Before her powers failed altogether she had perceived the presence of the stone-demon, and how through it the harracks could control the very rock itself, fault and vein. Wasting away, she lost all track of time, oppressed by the darkness and in peril of losing even her sanity. This was how Curillian had found her: weak, shrunken, beyond all hope. The red warrior from her past had reappeared and borne her back into the light. Only it wasn't really light at first, for the darkness clung to her even after she came into the open air again. She remembered the onset of great danger and trying to summon her powers against it, only to be constrained. Then there was a blank that she remembered not at all, and even after the stone-demon's fall, there was deep vagueness in her mind about their escape.

In fact, she recalled little until the snow-elves started to minister to her. With their arts, she was brought back to herself, and a little strength was imbued into her gaunt frame. Retrieved from the brink of forgetfulness, her spirit resumed its rightful place and the rest of her being soon followed. Yet not until now, with the rising of the sun on a clear morning, had the last of the darkness been washed away.

'Now I feel strong again; now many pathways lie open to me.' She looked at him and the vision of her tale receded. He saw her smile, brilliant in the sunlight, and his heart was warmed.

'I wanted to ask…how it was that you came to be trapped.'

'And now you know. You've come to my rescue before, Ruthion, but never again, my heart tells me. The former days are gone, and time hurries on to a new age. I cherish this time alone, for we shall never have it again. Very soon our paths shall sunder, we who were once comrades-in-arms for Prélan. Who knows wither He will lead you and I in the end? But now? Now it is my turn to come to your rescue, for your quest threatens to fail before it has begun. Follow the river below you until you come to the Eldarell Water-Meadows. There you shall have the audience that you need. See? I go ahead of you...'

Before his eyes, she changed. Casting off her raiment, she exchanged her skin for feathers and her arms for wings. With one last look, she unfolded her falcon's wings and launched herself from that promontory. With a keening cry, she soared over the wide valley below and was lost in the golden haze of the sun. The tug on Curillian's heart was so strong that he nearly leapt after her, but he gripped the edge of the rock and held himself tight. For a long time he watched after her, pangs of loss welling up inside him. In the confusion of his heart, he did not know what he had lost. A comrade? A friend? A lover? His memories cheated him so that he could not look back and clearly recall their encounters; all was lost in a blissful haze. He tried to leave the giddiness of those emotions behind on the high rock place, but in his climb down, he was heavy of heart. Yet when he reached the bottom of the outcrop, he perceived a door opening up before him, and an avenue closed and hidden behind him.

A

'Where is the princess?' Roujeark asked as Curillian returned to the camp. The rest were up now, assembling a breakfast round the cooking-fire, but they all stopped to look at him as he drew near. Each one marked something strange about the king, though to each of them it seemed different.

'She has gone ahead,' Curillian answered, 'to prepare the way.' Lancoir gave him a strange look, but no more was said. As they broke the camp, Curillian enquired of Sin-Serin.

'We are near to our goal now?'

'Verily,' affirmed the elf, 'the Spring of Eldaphir is near.'

'Good,' said Curillian. Then, turning to his armist companions, he told them, 'Our toiling in the foothills is at an end; soon we shall descend into the Vale of Nimrell.'

They spent one last night in the high country, exposed and cold. They built up a fire and, out of deference to Sin-Serin, went to the toil of scouring far and wide for wood that was dead. The wood-elf left them to their own devices, slipping off into the night. So the six armists were left alone.

'Come,' said Curillian. 'We only have the cordial of the snow-elves, but let us toast our fallen comrades.' They all stood. Curillian pronounced the roll call of honour. 'Haroth, and Manrion, who were lost in the avalanche.'

'They did their duty,' Lancoir intoned. 'Prélan keep their warrior's souls.' They drank.

'Cyron, Edrist, Norscinde and Utarion, slain by the bridge's collapse.'

'They did their duty; Prélan keep their warrior's souls.' This time they all chorused the words with their captain. They drank again, and, in unison, they tipped the last measure of their cups into the fire. It rushed up in sudden blue-white fury, and then settled back down, hissing and moaning.

'So there *was* something good in it after all,' said Aleinus wryly. Having satisfied honour, they sat down again around the fire. Curillian gazed into the flames awhile.

'Would that I could have brought them back home for a proper funeral.'

'Sire, they died happy,' said Findor. 'There's not an armist under arms in the land who wouldn't want to die in your service. They none of them had wives or children left behind. Their souls have gone to the right place, so what do the bodies matter?'

'And Haroth always sought a glorious death,' added Andil, who had been his friend. Lancoir, who had not spoken yet, now gave his verdict.

'His glory shall be that he died in courage, for he went where others dare not.' None seemed to care to add to the captain's words, and there was silence for a time. Then Curillian spoke again, lighter of heart.

'Ah, but you all fought well, my loyal guards. It is no small thing for you to have come through unscathed.' They all nursed cuts and bruises, but grinned nonetheless. 'The deeds of those on this expedition will be sung with praise in the palace and the academy, but great indeed shall be your renown if you live through what is yet to come. The armists who infiltrated Faudunum and came out alive, who went on to compete in the Great Tournament at Oron Amular? Centuries shall come and go and still such prestige shall remain undimmed. And what about you, friend Roujeark? Very glad I am that you were with us. You grow mightier with each passing fight.' Roujeark blushed and looked at his hands. They had not been scorched this time, though the flames had burned hotter, and been sustained longer.

'When I first met you,' Lancoir said, 'I despised you for a peasant weakling. Yet soon you will prove harder to kill than I.' Roujeark looked up at the Captain of the Guard and shivered. Such a compliment was not lightly given. He pulled his cloak tighter about him.

'Then let the other contestants beware,' exclaimed Caréysin. 'For Knights of Thainen are hard enough to kill.'

'It is not the other contestants you need worry about,' said Curillian. 'The Keeper of the Mountain will likely prove a sterner test than they. Prélan only knows how long Kulothiel has been preparing the tournament ground. We shall be competing in a mountain-kingdom that was already ancient when our race first awoke. We shall enter into halls where the deadliest weapons known to history were made and the most subtle minds trained. Every artifice and device contrived by the elven mages throughout the depths of time shall be deployed between us and the prize. Elves and men and armists shall compete, but the Mountain itself will be our foe.' There was silence again, as each armist contemplated the king's words in the flames.

'What of the harracks?' Antaya asked at length. 'Will they be there to compete?'

'No, I do not think so,' the king answered. 'They have longed to discover the Mountain and conquer it too long to be given an invitation. You have seen your last of them, I hope.'

'I've crossed blades with them,' pressed Antaya, 'and yet I still do not have it clear in my mind what they are. Do they have souls, or are they beasts?'

'No one knows for sure,' answered the king. 'When we first encountered them, they were already at odds with our people, so all we have learned of them we have discerned from afar as enemies. Beasts? I think not – they are too skilled in craft for that.'

'Some of their architecture was very impressive,' Roujeark offered.

'Indeed,' agreed the king. 'As shapers of stone and delvers of mines they have few equals, which lends credence to the theories that they are degenerate dwarves, sundered from the kin of Carthak long ago and fallen into evil, like the Black Dwarves of the Goragath Mountains. They are even more secretive than the dwarves, adept at concealment and camouflage, but they have shown no evidence of the dwarves' nobler arts: runes and literature, and the fashioning of gems and marvellous works of skill. We may never know who or what they are. I count them enemies as long as they menace my realm, but I will never hunt them without cause as things not worthy of life.'

One by one, the armists fell asleep around the fire, until only Roujeark was awake. His mind struggled as the implications of what he had done amongst the harracks sank in. He had taken life, and taken it with ease. He sensed tremendous power within himself, and it frightened him. He almost longed for the doubts that had once wracked him, for at least he did not need to guard others from them. *Who am I? What will I become?*

'You are learning to control it,' a deep voice spoke from across the fire. Roujeark looked up, startled. So long had he been gazing at the fire that it took his eyes some time to adjust and discern Curillian beyond, not slumbering as he had thought. The king's voice was thick with the authority of discernment.

'When my father said I had the same gift as he, I thought I might be able to move small objects, or create fleeting lights. I never saw my father do what I have now done.'

'Your father did not face danger as you have, nor fight alongside comrades whose plight would move him to greater things than he had known before. I do not know if magical ability is hereditary, but I do know that it is a gift of Prélan, bestowed by His Spirit where He wills it to be. He has bestowed it on you. And for a reason.'

'Am I to be a killer then?'

Curillian hesitated. 'Everyone feels remorse after their first killing. The barbarians who crossed you back in the Phirmar probably died, but this time it is certain. Moreover, back then what came from your fingertips was wild and undirected; now it is becoming harnessed and deadly.' Curillian saw the young armist was unconvinced, full of confusion. 'Roujeark, the first person I killed was, like yours, out of necessity.'

A distant look came into the king's eyes as he recalled that far off day.

'Do not torment yourself over death in battle,' he went on. 'For everyone present has embraced it as a possibility. The harracks would feel no guilt in slaying you, for even now they would be melting the skin off your bones had you not denied them. You killed only to defend your friends. If Prélan has called us to nothing else, He has called us to love, and, if necessary, to give our lives for those we love. Listen to me: I have been given many gifts in my life, and all of them to a purpose. It will be the same with you.'

'What purpose?'

'Roujeark, the wizards are gone. Their mighty deeds belong to the pages of history now. Kulothiel may well be the only one left. And now another has arisen? Why would Prélan call forth such a one unless for an errand of surpassing greatness?'

Curillian stood up, stretched, and walked around the fire. He looked down at the seated Roujeark. 'My young friend, all I can say is what is plain to my eyes. I have not lived so long by being blind to what is before them. Yet it may well be that you will not get your answers until you get to Oron Amular, so you must be patient. My task is simply to get you there.' He squeezed his young companion's shoulder. 'Now, let me see if I can find our elf...' With that, he strode off into the night.

⚔

The elf had not gone far, for she was still with them in the morning. If she had scouted through the night, she had found what he sought for. That very day they left the mountain glens behind and descended into an eastward-plunging valley. The top of the valley was marked by a window of rock, through which trickled a gurgle of water. *Eldaphir's Spring.* Unmistakeably the trickle grew into a stony stream, carving its way downhill. All they did was follow. It dropped steeply down, taking them to warmth and fecundity. Sin-Serin laughed with sheer joy and ran dancing on ahead, to the bemusement of her travelling companions. This was the first time they had seen their grim guide like this, joyful and carefree. It gladdened their own hearts to behold it.

'My friends,' interpreted Curillian. 'Though you may not be transported to such delight as our guide, do you not feel it in your feet? We tread now on immortal grass, for we are come to Kalimar. It would go ill for us if we came here uninvited, but do not fear, we have one to vouch for us. Ah, truly, it is only now that my weariness falls from me...'

They lost sight of Sin-Serin and walked on for a time without her through fields of fragrant early wildflowers. Full springtime was burgeoning around them. Birds and butterflies, brighter than they had ever seen, darted and sang all about them. They were passing a forest on the far bank when their guide called to them. Looking across, they saw her sitting at leisure on the green bank under branches that overhung the stream. Her foot rested carelessly on the prow of a long slim rowboat.

'Friends, worry no longer about your aching feet, for we have been given alternative means of transport. Our coming was known, and folk were waiting with this boat, here, where Eldaphir first becomes deep enough to bear one.'

The armists looked around, but they could see no one. Roujeark thought he could hear laughter off among the trees, but it might have been only the wind. Still, the boat looked sturdy enough, and larger than expected, for when Sin-Serin brought it across to them, nimble as an otter, they found it had plenty of room for all ten of them and what remained of their packs. So they continued on their way by water, now paddling, now drifting with the current through lands as lovely as a dream. The air was warm and still. Summer was not far off. They relaxed under sunny skies and watched the peaceful banks slide by with their willows and alders. When Roujeark dangled his arm over the side, his fingers grazed the waters of the shallow stream and felt them almost warm to the touch.

The stream grew wider and deeper, meandering through places where the trees grew densely on either bank. For a time they seemed to be gliding through an enchanting tunnel where the leaves above and the waters below joined in a hundred wondrous shades of green.

'Where are we bound?' Roujeark asked. Curillian looked back over his shoulder to answer as he helped paddle.

'To the Eldarell Water-Meadows.' The name meant nothing to any of them, and indeed, Curillian himself had never been there. He leaned forward to Sin-Serin, who paddled from the prow.

'How far off are we?'

'Soon we shall come to where Eldaphir joins Nimrell, her cousin. Then we shall be but half a day's journey as the river will take us.'

'What waits for us there?' Lionenn called from the stern of the boat, his voice uneasy.

'You will see,' Curillian answered.

Just as the wood-elf had said, they came to the confluence where the small Eldaphir joined the larger Nimrell River. Curillian knew enough Kalimari geography to know that the Nimrell was one of the great waterways of Kalimar. Here they were, still well above where the valley's main habitations started, and the river had hundreds of miles to go before emptying into her namesake bay, whose waters also lapped a tiny part of Maristonia's eastern coast. Yet the Nimrell was already a great river. She was sprung from a hundred streams, which tumbled down from snowfields in the mountains. As they swung into the main channel, they could look back and see those mountains clearly for the first time. The mighty peaks, glistening in the distance, were beautiful to behold, and Roujeark wondered whether they were as tall as the Carthaki Mountains whose shadow he had grown up in. Yet for all the youthful vigour of the mountain waters, the Nimrell here entered into a sluggish stretch, spreading out in wide meanders as the valley floor swiftly broadened out. They passed many small lakes beside the banks, and saw wide watery floodplains extending on either side. Herons stalked, swallows wheeled and warblers burbled amid the reeds.

They paused to make camp for the night, and resumed on their way in the morning. Sin-Serin had them up and going very early, while mists still clung to the river. Flotillas of giant swans were there only companions. Sin-Serin surely chose this hour knowingly, for the place they came to seemed achingly lovely at this hour. The river gave out into broad meadows where multiple channels wended their way lazily. Clumps of reeds grew up, and little tree-clad hillocks poked up out of the waters. The mists slowly burned off as soft sunlight dappled the peaceful world. The only noise was that of the birds all around them. Fish seemed abundant and waterfowl fluttered about, ducks, geese and waders in great numbers. Again, the armists never saw a sign, but Sin-Serin told them, 'The Avatar are all around us.'

The name made Roujeark nervous, for it reminded him of the fierce riders who had tried to expel him from the land when he first came to Kalimar. A higher power had turned their eyes away on that occasion, but this time Roujeark did not know what to expect. Sin-Serin too seemed slightly less at ease, for while the Avatar were elves also, they were a kindred distinct from the Firnai wood-elves.

'The Avatar,' began Curillian, answering unvoiced questions, 'are a high and excellent people, but they are perilous and jealous of their realm. Leave the talking to myself and Sin-Serin.' A strange air of nervous expectancy settled over them, and even the quacking and honking of the birds seemed to subside.

'Behold,' said Sin-Serin, suddenly and softly. 'Your rendezvous approaches.' They all looked out into the hazy light, but could see nothing but huge dragonflies skimming above the water. Several moments passed before the sharp-eyed Caréysin called out and nudged his companions.

'Look, there, coming through the mists.'

They followed his pointing arm, and there, sure enough, coming through the mists, was a large waterborne conveyance. It was a vast raft, serenely guided through the water meadows by silent, golden-haired puntsmen. The details only slowly became apparent, but it was obvious that this was no common vessel. As comely and well-built as it was large, it was fit for a king. Devices of a six-pointed star were held aloft on shields and banners by silent sentinels, still as statues. The raft shimmered with the reflected light of precious metals and stones as it glided towards them. Many persons were on the raft: four puntsmen, one at each corner, and stern warriors watching out. A group of people stood near the middle, but the spellbound armists had eyes only for the spectacular figure seated on a throne at the very centre. This person was taller seated than any of those standing around him and, though he wore no crown, his bearing and countenance was regal.

Curillian was taken aback to see Lithan, High King of the elves, drawing near. He was not sure whom he had expected, but it had certainly not been the ruler of Kalimar. Here was a being who had been alive for over two and a half thousand years, and who was yet considered young among his kindred. Descended directly from the Elder King, Avatar himself, six generations distant, Lithan was the last scion of the House of Avatar to remain in Kalimar. In all his adventures, Curillian had never come within sight of him. He had met his older cousin, Lancearon, when he was still the Silver Emperor, but as awe-inspiring as Lancearon was, he was a very worldly elf, monarch after a pattern recognisable to mortal eyes. Lithan was very different. He was set apart, ethereal and aloof, and the grace of the elder line of Avatar's dynasty was in his face.

Even more so than Curillian, the other armists were spellbound as their boat nudged alongside the great raft and they were beckoned aboard. None of the other elves batted an eyelid as they assembled clumsily before the throne, and High King Lithan sat still as a carven statue. It was a voice coming from behind the throne that welcomed them, and it was a voice they knew.

'Welcome, and twice-met, warriors from afar.'

Carea stepped into view. While her voice had been recognisable, the rest of her was completely changed. The elf-lady they had parted with only days before had been a pale, dark-cloaked waif, tired and weak; but now there stood before them a tall, radiant queen. And they were dazzled. Health and vitality, such as a mortal could never hope to possess, shone in her face, and the beauty that had before been shrouded now smote them like the noonday sun. With familiar courtesy, she introduced them to the High King.

'Armists of Maristonia, behold His Grace the High King of Kalimar, Lithan, son of Avalar, chieftain of the Avatar and overlord of all elves.' The armists went to one knee before him. 'Lord King, see here your neighbour and brother-king, Curillian of Maristonia, of the House of Carinen. By his side stand Lancoir, Captain of the Royal Guards of Mariston, and his valiant comrades-in-arms, Aleinus, Antaya, Findor, Andil, Caréysin and Lionenn. With them stands Roujeark, the last pupil-elect of Kulothiel.'

As she spoke the words of introduction, it was as if a spell had been lifted from Lithan, for his grave regal countenance broke and he leaned forward with a welcoming smile upon his lips. He rose from his throne and stood by Curillian as he returned to his feet. If the armists had thought he was tall while he was still seated, they now saw that he was fully eight feet tall. He towered over Curillian. The armist king was the tallest of his companions, but still he only came level with Lithan's breast. The elven king laid hands upon his shoulders.

'How is it, valiant Curillian, that it is only now that we meet? For all the mighty deeds of your ancestors, yours surely is the greatest renown. Verily, our realms have drifted apart with time, but I bear you no less love than your forebears.'

'Majesty, the honour is mine,' Curillian responded, his words sounding awkward in his own ears after Lithan's lordly tones. 'Glad I am to have met you, O High King, but I have never presumed upon an invitation.'

Lithan moved on from Curillian, but while he acknowledged all the others, and embraced Sin-Serin as a cherished kinself, he did not pass over Roujeark as the young armist had expected. Roujeark was startled and abashed when the elven High King crouched in front of him so that their eyes were more or less level.

'My young friend, you are certainly not the least welcome here. Twice now have you come to my kingdom, but only now do I bid you welcome. My riders thought nothing of it when you vanished forty suns ago, but clearly, Prélan was at work in our land that night. I am not so privy to the counsels of the League as were my fathers, but I still know that your coming was foretold.' He straightened up to tower over them again.

'Curillian, son of Mirkan, you come to me via a strange path. Do I not guess rightly that you are bound for Oron Amular?'

'I am, Your Grace.'

'Evidently you chose not to ride the straight road, which would have brought you to my home, but instead emerge from the mountains bearing gifts unlooked for. Prélan, it seems, has ordained it so. Had you come to Paeyeir, even with an escort, you would have been welcome, for Kulothiel requested that I hinder not the invited who came peacefully, but I could have done no more; it was for each contestant to find the road to the Mountain without aid. Come, elf-friend, ask your boon.'

Curillian looked to Carea, who smiled, and then up to the elven king.

'Your Grace, I request passage to Oron Amular, and ask your leave to pass freely through your domain.' Lithan looked down on him with kingly pleasure.

'It is granted full willing, Curillian of Mariston. You are a noble and excellent armist, descended from a house of elf-friends, and held in high esteem by my cousin, Lancearon; for these reasons alone, you have claim upon me. But now, you come with even more potent persuasion, for you have rescued Carea, daughter of Therendir, she who is even more senior in her house than I am in mine. She was lost, and feared dead, but you have brought her forth out of the cold shadows. All of Kalimar, and the House of Firnar in especial, is indebted to you, heroic descendent of a blesséd house.'

'You are kinder than I deserve, O High King,' said Curillian, bowing low. Lithan proved to be kinder still, for he invited them to eat with him upon his raft. Surrounded by the beauty of the water meadows, they broke their fast upon warm loaves, divinely soft and fragrant. The fruits they ate were so flavourful that they could scarce believe they were the same as those that they knew in their own country, and the hibiscus flowers steeped in clear elven cordial was so refreshing that they quite forgot the toils they had come through. After they had eaten, more of the same foods were bestowed on them in generous packets to take with them for the road. As they retired replete from the table, Lithan declared a further kindness to them.

'It is my wish to bless you with the loan of horses, and furthermore, I consent to escort you to the start of your path. The young wizard, I believe,' he said, turning to Roujeark, 'knows the lost way to Oron Amular which starts in the Aravell Valley.' Roujeark nodded nervously. 'If he can remember his steps, then you will come to Kulothiel's hidden gates. Should the Keeper think I have helped you too well, he will indulge his liege-lord, for my thankfulness for the deliverance of Carea outweighs my willingness to abide by his wishes.'

Sin-Serin and Carea took their leave of the armists then, for their time had come to return to Tol Ankil, where Dácariel waited for them. Carea made her thanks to each of her rescuers, kissing them farewell. Sin-Serin laid his forehead against Curillian's, and they too exchanged farewells.

'My thanks to you, Sin-Serin, daughter of the forest. You have been a good guide to us.' Last of all, Curillian went to one knee before Carea, and kissed her hand tenderly. She smiled on him.

'Farewell, and Prélan bless you, Ruthion-Curillian, comrade and friend. If ever we meet again, it shall not be for long, and the tides of providence will bear us apart. Yet my friendship to you shall endure beyond the confines of this world. In the meantime, I shall repay the last of my debt to you by preparing the help you will need.' With those words, she was gone, and none of those that looked on knew what a painful parting they had just witnessed.

Lithan gave orders for the raft to clear the water meadows and make landfall on the eastern bank, where horses were waiting. None of the armists saw where the two wood-elves went, though when he turned back, Roujeark saw two waterbucks leaping gracefully through the watery tracks. He blinked, not sure if he had seen aright, but all he saw when he re-opened his eyes were two wild horses on the distant western bank, running strongly south.

＊

VI

Retracing Red Steps

HORSES Were waiting on the banks beyond the water meadows, the same horses which had borne Lithan and his entourage in haste from Paeyeir, the Kalimari capital. Spare mounts had been purposefully brought, and these were now given over to the armists, their stirrups already shortened ready for them. With little delay, they rode away, following the eastern bank of the Nimrell downstream. Coming to one of the great river's tributaries, they rode upstream until they found a ford. Once across, they left the river valley behind and rode across rolling green hills. In two days' gentle riding, they came to the crest of a steep ridge and, looking down, beheld the Aravell valley. This valley neighboured the Nimrell, and it marked the very heartland of Kalimar. Across the river rose a mighty hill, surrounded by a spherical forest, and upon whose summit sat a fair city. Thus, they became the first mortals for many years to behold Avarianmar, the demesne of the High King of the elves, and Paeyeir, his ancient ancestral abode. Pale and graceful as a thicket of frosted saplings, its many towers, gables and domes glimmered in the westering sunshine, and its banners danced in the breeze.

The armists sat in their saddles and gaped at the sight; even Curillian had never seen this. However, Roujeark had, if not from this vantage point. His eye was drawn to the road, which crossed the river, ran through the forest and climbed up the hill to the city, the very same road whose western reaches he had walked before. The

Armist Road, whose one end was used by armists, and whose other served the elves, was the oldest highway in Astrom. Then he turned his eye to the great stone bridge by which the road crossed the Aravell. He was taken back to the day when, after being smuggled through the immortal lands, he was set down at that bridge to continue his quest for Oron Amular. Now, forty years later, he was on the same quest again. Would he enter the Mountain this time? Or would he be turned away a second time?

Following Lithan's lead, they left the ridge-top behind, and followed a small stream down into the valley. Keeping parallel to the great road, they intersected the river a few furlongs upstream from the bridge. As Lithan rode up to his armist guests on his great white horse, they knew the time had come for parting. As one, the armists looked longingly to the place where the road plunged into the immortal forest, wishing they could follow it up to the mythical capital, of which so many tales and legends told. Instead, the High King gestured upstream, to where the Aravell hugged the forest as it climbed slowly up into the highlands.

'My adventurous friends, the time has come for us to part. Our time together has been brief, but full of pleasure. I go back now to my halls, but your way leads up into the mountains. It is time for your guide to come to the fore and play his part. With Prélan's blessing, I leave you in his capable hands.'

They bade the elven king farewell with fitting words, and surrendered their borrowed mounts to the grooms who had ridden with them. They watched as king, grooms and knights, the whole royal entourage, rode down and across the bridge. In a flurry of hooves and streaming pennons, they vanished into the forest as if it were a portal that took them to another time and place. They were left alone, elf-less for the first time since coming to Tol Ankil. As they had left Mariston, so now they would go on, a company of armists.

Curillian was just about to address Roujeark when the young armist hurried off, running in the direction of the bridge. Fearing lest he might outstep the bounds of their welcome, the king called after him, but he was gone.

'Shall we fetch him back, Curillian?' Lancoir asked. The king watched the receding red figure, red cloak flying.

'No, he is called.'

Roujeark ran as close as he dared to the bridge, mindful of the sentries who stood there, and then he scrambled down into the reeds on the bank and crept the rest of the way into the shadow of the great stone arch. He had come here once before to meet Prélan, and by Prélan's grace, he had been left unmolested. He trusted to that protection again now, and settled himself down between the water and the stone. Everything seemed different. Last time it had been night; now it was daytime. Last time strange characters in the river had lit the underside of the bridge with luminous instructions; now the water was dark and still. Last time he had heard Prélan's voice speak to him; now all was quiet.

He tried to concentrate his mind to hear Prélan, but his thoughts were in turmoil. A frustration grew in him that made him squirm and fidget where he sat. Finally, despairing of hearing anything as he gazed into the river, he looked around. As he did so, a memory came to him of words spoken long ago…

Now, it is right for me to give you this, to light the next steps…

They were the words of Ardir, the angelic being from whose hand he had received the living map that showed the way to Oron Amular. Why didn't I think of that before, he wondered? Suddenly excited, he reached into his innermost pocket and drew forth the map. It was his most treasured possession, even though he didn't look at it very often. He lovingly unwrapped the leather bindings, and opened up the parchment within. His heart sank immediately. That's why I didn't think of it: it's blank. It had been like that when he first received it, and it only began to reveal itself when his feet found the right path. As he went, it had confirmed his route by remaining blank when he was astray, and only filling in when he was on the right track.

He remembered the time when he had come within sight of Oron Amular. The whole map had been revealed, a stunning tapestry of colour so richly textured that it was as if the land itself had been captured inside it. The path he had trodden showed, in a stippled red line. A red line for a red wanderer. *Rutharth*, Red Journey, indeed. He had put it away when he had retraced his steps back to Maristonia, for it showed not that land. Somewhere along the line, as it lay unread against his skin, it had reverted to its original state, blankness reclaiming the paper like desert sands engulfing an oasis. The first time he had discovered the loss the blow had smote his heart, for he had counted on using it to find the way back some day.

It is not as other maps, made to quench the beholder's curiosity all at once; yet nevertheless, it will guide you true, step by step.

Ardir's other words winged into his mind as he sat wracked by doubt. The revelation that followed struck him like a stone on the forehead. Would it happen the same way again? Would the map come alive again if he found the right path?

Trust in Prélan and He will not lead you astray...

Roujeark realised he had all he needed after all. His memories of the journey first time around were only vague, but he felt sure that they would become clearer when he came back to each place in turn, especially if the map helped him again. Pushing himself up on his haunches, he clasped the map tight against his chest.

Prélan, guide my steps, he prayed. *Help me retrace my steps. Take me to the Mountain. Let me enter in this time, and ascend, that I might meet with You again.*

His companions were restless and impatient by the time he rejoined them.

'Right,' he told them. 'Follow me.'

A

Packs hoisted and boot-laces drawn tight, they trekked up the river bank. For a time, while the forest hugged the bank, they felt like they were being watched. Yet soon they reached a fork in the river. The forest arched away northward, following the right-hand channel; whilst the left-hand way curved away to the left into quiet green country. Roujeark remembered taking the left-hand way here before. That had been before he had received the map, which came to him when he gained the hills higher up, but he saw now that the map backed up his memory. In its bottom-right corner, it flushed suddenly and showed the confluence in the river. Yet while the right-hand river was immediately lost over its edge, the left-hand way was illuminated as it crept diagonally up across the parchment. Delighted, he made haste to follow.

⟁

For days they wound their way up the river valley through a quiet and empty land. They passed through woods and splashed over fords across side-streams, but always they followed the main river. One day they scaled a steep bluff beside the river and found that they had reached a similar vantage point to the ridgetop where, in the High King's company, they had looked out over Paeyeir and Avarianmar. Now at the same height, they could see the royal elven city again, rising on its hill clear of the surrounding forest, only this time they viewed it from the west, as opposed to the south. They also saw, much closer to them, that the other river was very nearby, only separated from them by a narrow ridge of intervening land. The two waterways flowed south through the land together, staying close as brothers unwilling to be parted. They came down from the same highlands, which, turning north-west, they could now clearly descry. Somewhere up ahead, the green grass and shady copses of lowland Kalimar gave way to more rugged heaths and moorland and beyond them, on the horizon, rose craggy hills and plateaus. The view, long forgotten in Roujeark's memory, now came back to mind as fresh and familiar as if it had never gone away.

Knowing he had to reach those uplands, Roujeark kept following the river. Curillian, Lancoir and the guards followed him without question. Now that they had left the watchful forest behind they felt more at ease, alone and untroubled. They took delight in each new flower and butterfly they saw, but kept going, up and up. They made cheerful fires by night, and sang songs and told stories by day to pass the long hours of trudging. Curillian had a great store of wonderful tales to share, great events that he himself had lived through or participated in. His companions drank up every word, though in the telling of those long-ago deeds he seemed as old to them as the land around them. Roujeark ignored one side-stream after another, sticking to the main channel, but then he came to a confluence where he could not tell which branch was the main river and which the tributary. His memory failed him here, so he struck out left with a guess. He had not gone far, however, before it became clear that he had left the map behind at the junction. They were walking in a blank section. Abruptly he turned around and, somewhat to his companions' alarm, led them back to the junction. He tried again, following the right-hand channel, and this time the map went with him, revealing a narrow strip along the valley.

Every night he took the map out and contemplated it, though he was careful never to let his companions see it. For a reason he knew not why, he wished to keep it to himself. The next day, walking through terrain that was noticeably hillier, the hairs on his neck began to prickle. The country, which for so long had seemed devoid of life, no longer felt quite so empty. Several sensations in his body were trying to tell him that he was coming to a significant place. Casting his mind back, he thought the hidden city he had discovered last time was nearby. He had discovered it quite by accident, and never found out its name or history, but the memory of it stood out clear amid mists of vagueness on either side.

He was out ahead of his companions when he stopped dead in his tracks. Barring the way ahead of him, standing as still as a statue, was an elf warrior. Resplendent in the armour and weaponry of an Avatar prince, he looked like he had stepped right out of the pages of history. His head was bowed and both hands were at rest on an upturned great-sword in front of him. Behind him, the riverbanks reared up in canyon walls through which the water tumbled frothily. As Roujeark gaped at him, the warrior raised his head and transfixed him with a terrifying glare, though he could see little through the gaps in the ornate helmet. Lifting one gauntleted hand, he pointed westward, away from the river and up the bank to one side. So intimidated was Roujeark that he let out a little cry and turned to his companions, who came hurrying up behind him. They asked what had startled him, but when he looked back upstream, the forbidding figure had vanished. Where he had stood, his sword alone remained, thrust point-ward into the turf. The guards fingered their weapons nervously. Fascinated, Curillian started towards the abandoned weapon.

'I think we should leave the river now,' Roujeark said nervously. Curillian went on a step or two and then came to a stop, hand resting on the hilt of his own sword. Then he retreated.

'Our way is barred,' he whispered to Roujeark. 'Let us find another route.'

Together they climbed away from the riverbank, up onto the shoulders of the canyon, which heralded the start of the hills. To Roujeark's relief, the map approved of their deviation from the river, divulging details of a narrow corridor through this mysterious land. They picked a way up the slope among moss-covered boulders and straggling trees. As they climbed, the churning thunder of the river down below receded, and they came into beech-woods perched above the canyon. Caution dictated a route on through the trees, but curiosity tugged Roujeark towards the canyon rim. He wandered off in that direction, but a sight in the trees brought him up short. His breath caught in his throat. A well-camouflaged figure perched on a branch in a tree forty yards from him. The menacing hooded figure held up a gloved hand, palm outward in a gesture of rejection. Then he drew his bow and crouched poised, ready to release. Roujeark caught a glimpse of baleful eyes from under the rim of the hood that chilled his heart. Stumbling backward, he returned to his original course.

His companions had seen nothing, and they followed his abortive detour away from, and then back to, their original course. They might have asked questions, but strange noises sounded in the trees, and they felt none too safe. They hurried on. A little further on, a break in the land lay across their path where a tributary of the river had carved a fern-filled side canyon. Roujeark led them down into the moist green cleft in search of a place to cross to the other side. His companions were strung out on the steep slope above him when he strayed too near the main river below. A dripping figure emerged out of the river. Clad in scaly blue and white, he was virtually invisible amongst the foam and boulders of some rapids. Crouching in a martial stance, he brandished a trident drawn back on a taut arm. The other hand was held out rigidly towards him in the same palm-outward gesture of denial. Roujeark stumbled back in fright and lost his footing. Again, the guards saw nothing, but the vigilant Curillian was quickly at his side.

'What is it?' he hissed. The guardian of the river had disappeared, but Roujeark was pale with fright.

'Nothing,' he told the king, and hurried to get up and move on. Going on from there, his heart barely stopped pounding all day. None of these apparitions had been there before, nor did he remember the canyon. He could not remember when or why he had left the river first time round, but he surmised sketchily that he must have followed a course off to the side. They spent an uneasy night under the trees, keeping their weapons close.

A

The next day a strange prompting roused him early. He left the guards still sleeping and crept off into the dawn half-light. Soon he was aware of Curillian coming with him. They looked at each other strangely.

'You feel it too?' the king asked him, but Roujeark did not know what to say. Together they followed their feet to an out-jutting promontory. Feeling increasingly nervous as they approached an overhang, they got down first to hands and knees, and then flat on their bellies. Crawling, they came to the edge and peered out over. A hidden world lay beneath them, now exposed. Elemental forces from a forgotten age had carved a vast amphitheatre in the hillside, and now it was filled with a marvellous city, like a jewel in a hollow. Out of morning mists, tall houses and needle-thin towers rose like icicles. Elegant arches supported domes and spires, from which issued soft and beautiful lights, like undying lamps. They glimpsed unkempt gardens and channelled waters flowing under graceful bridges. All of it bespoke the finest architecture of the Avatar, the High Elves, the finest builders ever to labour above the earth. Fascinating suburbs delved into the sheer sides of the amphitheatre and some dwellings even clung to the very rock faces. A river emerged out of a rocky tunnel on one side, wound its way through the city, and then departed southward by another tunnel. The whole place was sealed off on all sides, invisible except from above.

And it was deserted.

Not a single soul was in sight. No traders sold their wares in the market squares, no horses' hooves clattered down the paved streets, and no gardeners tended the neglected and overgrown lawns. Not even wild animals haunted this place. Forgotten by the outside world, the city seemed to have forgotten itself. If the three apparitions had been guarding this city, it was a dead place they watched over. Nature was trying to reclaim the place with groping roots and spreading briers, but the buildings themselves had a timeless quality, as if their makers had intended them to stand until the end of days, even though they themselves should depart.

'This is Aramar,' whispered Curillian beside him. As the first fingers of dawn touched the tallest turrets with rosy hues, there was a look of rapture in his face. The name flittered at the back of Roujeark's mind, as if trying to elicit a long-forgotten memory, but Curillian evidently knew more.

'Roujeark, do you realise? We've come to a place where our kind has never been before – we're looking at a fabled city which no armist eyes have ever beheld. And yet, the beginnings of our history are bound up with this place, for from this ancient citadel of the elves came the host which first settled Maristonia, centuries before my forefathers first awoke. Aramar. City of Arvaya, Avar, and Arvarion. City of many kings. Birthplace and home to many generations of Avatar's elder line, and a place that once rivalled Paeyeir as the capital of Kalimar. The folk here used to be called the deep-elves, the Irynthai. It was one of the fairest cities of the elves, and one of the most industrious too, for many fine things were invented or discovered here.

'Kurundar lusted after it so much that, although he lacked the strength to invade Kalimar properly in the Second War, he sent a special taskforce to sack it. Whilst I fought in the west, we heard tales that the fabled city of Aramar had been besieged. It remained so until the ending of the war, at the dawn of the Fourth Chapter. Avallonë, King of Kalimar at the time, and father of Lithan, whom you have met, died defending his gates, but he preserved the home of his fathers. Much damage was said to have been done, and most of its folk departed to the Inner Isles, despairing of the war-torn homes they had lost, but some stayed, and rebuilt it in the image of its former glory. They rebuilt it, and then they too left, for as you see, the city lies deserted. Now it is naught but a memorial to the ancient greatness of the Avatar.'

Roujeark, who had known none of this, listened with rapt attention. Curillian had more to tell.

'It was the most secretive part of Kalimar, save Oron Amular itself. Foreign ambassadors and embassies might come to Paeyeir, down in the lowlands, but none were ever permitted to come to this place – it was kept sacred. And so, we are the first mortals to ever see it, what some have deemed to be a lost treasure. Some even doubted that it had ever existed, save in song and legend only. I never doubted, but I listened to the stories like everyone else. One particular legend told of three guardians who were left behind by the departing population to guard it.'

Roujeark stirred, and looked at Curillian keenly.

'An Avatar, a Firnar, and a Marintor, brothers-in-arms representing all three kindreds,' the king went on. 'It is said that they watch over the approaches to this city with sword, bow and trident, and suffer none to pass. Theirs was a solemn and eternal duty: to preserve the inviolate mystery and serenity of Aramar, city of elven dreams. That tale I did not believe, until now. I think you saw these three watchers, Roujeark, even though none of the rest of us glimpsed them.'

'But why have we been allowed to come here, and look out over the city?' Roujeark asked, puzzled and nervous. He kept expecting the three to appear again, each in their own element.

'Who knows? Seeing is not trespassing, perhaps. We would never have been allowed to come to the city itself and set our feet upon it. There may come a day when men or armists try to venture here, seeking treasure and ancient lore, but even if the three guardians let them pass, it will be a perilous undertaking. The Irynthai were the most cunning of all elves, well able to booby-trap the city they had kept secret for so long. Yet we have the leave of the High King himself to come this way; you are beckoned by Prélan and drawn by a powerful doom. Notice how all of our companions slumber strangely on past daybreak? Their eyes have been closed, but ours are permitted to see. Roujeark, it sets my heart beating faster. If Aramar may be glimpsed, then who knows? Maybe even Oron Amular will give up her secrets…'

When they returned to their companions, they found them slumbering still, held in the grip of a strange drowsiness. When they were shaken awake, they seemed strangely vacant and unobservant of what was around them. Even Lancoir was lethargic. Roujeark and Curillian hurried them away from that secret place, and it was not until late afternoon, when they had left it far behind, that they became their usual selves again.

All that day and the next, they climbed up and up, coming across hillsides ever more barren and windswept. The trees were now almost exclusively evergreen, and they clung to the slopes in serried ranks. Roujeark searched for the cave that had been the setting for his third encounter with Prélan all those years ago, but it eluded him. He felt sure it would be nearby if he stuck to the correct path, for that had been the way he had come before, but he couldn't find it. Maybe he had taken a detour the first time that he didn't remember, or perhaps the fir-trees had colonised the cave-mouth in the years in between and hidden it. Or maybe the cave had been a secret portal to Prélan's own country, which, having served its purpose, had now been swallowed up by the earth and closed forever?

He did at least find the lake he had visited before, which they reached after much toiling and scrambling. He remembered the steep escarpment that rose behind it, and the flatter ground west of it, which he had been grateful to traverse instead. They had come far enough into the hills now that the lowlands were hidden, but they knew that the waters stored up here fed one of the great rivers of Kalimar, for out of the lake tumbled myriad little streams which gradually convened to form the Aravell.

They trod the wooded shores of the lake until they ended and then followed the buttress of higher ground above them. Low clouds and persistent rain dogged their steps for the next few days, and Roujeark feared going astray in the poor visibility, but he kept the high ground on his right like a guiding fence, and every time he checked the map, it reassured him that he was on course.

One morning they finally left the clinging clouds behind and, breasting a low crest which jutted above the plateau, they were given a spectacular view west and south. To left and right the northern and southern flanks of the plateau tumbled away gradually into the lowlands, but ahead of them lay the Black Mountains in all their glory. Stern dark masses of rock reared upwards like the shoulders of the world. Above they rose into jagged spires and fluted pyramids, and below the bitter cliffs and craggy flanks plunged away into dank labyrinthine networks of ravines and sunless clefts. Only the glistening snow covering the greatest peaks softened the forbidding prospect, like the flowing white hair that makes a grave elder seem somehow more benevolent. The sunlight glinted off that snow, and glittered among the ice-clad valleys where rivers birthed.

They had had a limited view of this range before, from the south, when they were in Aiiyosha's company, but now the view was untrammelled on any side, and it was as if the whole world lay spread out before them. Yet the mountains themselves were still many miles distant. Between themselves and those far-off peaks was a great flat-topped ridge, many miles broad, which jabbed out from the massif like a blunted blade. Following its long miles with their eyes, they tried to descry their path, but all they could see was a trackless wilderness of rock where no green thing grew. Roujeark strained his eyes westward, hoping for some glimpse of the Mountain, for he knew it stood apart from the others. But either he was looking in the wrong place, or the enormous peak was still too far distant to see, hidden behind nearer peaks. Disappointed, he returned to his job of path-finding.

Down they went, leaving the height behind and going back down to the plateau. That night they had their first glimpse of the moon for many days, and Curillian paused to take his bearings from it.

'The new moon rises,' he said. 'The last one of spring. The next full moon will be the first of summer, and the date set for the Tournament. That means we have only two weeks to reach the Mountain if we are to get there on time. How far away are we, Roujeark?'

But Roujeark did not know. He thought they were getting close now, but he could not even begin to put a guess in days on it. He was totally dependent on his enigmatic map, and the others were totally dependent on him. Curillian and his warrior escort learned a new appreciation for Roujeark in that place, knowing they would have become hopelessly lost without him. The great ridge was not as flat as it had looked from above, but instead was crumpled in folded ranks of troughs and outcrops. Prehistoric torments had riven and rent it with elemental forces, and numerous crevices scored deeply across their path.

So their going was tough, and their progress frustratingly slow. Even with the aid of his map, Roujeark still went wrong several times, and many days were lost in difficult detours and temper-fraying retraced steps. When they were sure of their direction they could still only go slowly, for the way was fraught with dangerous places where one of them could have plummeted into mysterious depths, never to be heard of again.

Roujeark consoled himself with the thought that the Mountain must be close now, for his first proper view of it had come whilst lost in terrain like this. He wondered how long it would be before they finally saw it. Wearily they hoped for a glimpse every day, just enough to reward their bone-jarring labours and spur them on with fresh impetus. But every day, they found their view cut off by looming outcrops of rock, or curtained off by thick clouds. In the meantime, they just kept trudging on, trying to ignore the growing number of blisters that made their steps increasingly painful. Their hardwearing mountain boots and cold-weather clothing was tested to the limits in that rugged wilderness, but they proved their worth, keeping them warm and much drier than they would otherwise have been.

Day by day, they forged on, encouraging each other by turns whenever one of them stumbled or tempers frayed. Still, at whiles Andil or Antaya would sing a few verses to keep their spirits up, and Aleinus told ridiculous jokes to keep them smiling. By night, they built fires whenever they came across wood, even if it was the gnarled limbs of wizened old pines crammed into some crevice. Taking sentry duty by turns, the rest of them reclined about the fire, getting as comfortable as they could in that desolate place. They kept close together and huddled under thick cloaks and blankets to keep out the mountain chill. Roujeark would discretely study his map or gaze at the stars. Curillian caressed Carmen's pendant and thought wistfully of home. He kept his wife and son ever in his prayers, and wondered from afar how Téthan was getting on. *He's been growing so fast these days. What a prince he would become one day.* His companions kept their own private thoughts or talked with each other, but Lancoir was ever restless, always whetting a blade on a rock or strolling about on patrol.

At the end of one long, soul-numbing day, they came to a rock-face that barred their way like a great ruined staircase. Vowing to find shelter as soon as possible on its far side, they drove themselves up the broken ledges and steps in half-light as evening fell. Leading as ever he did, Roujeark was the first to reach the top, and he came up short. Grasping the lip of the topmost step, he hauled himself up and found what he had been yearning for. Perfectly framed between two upward-jutting fingers of rock, like a window with no top, was a clear view to the north-west. The great Mountain, standing clear of the slopes beside her, dominated the view. Impossibly tall, snow-clad and starkly beautiful, the mightiest peak in Astrom was unmistakable. Oron Amular. Immeasurably loftier and incomparably fairer, it made the other bastions of the Black Mountains look like misshapen lumps. Standing upon a vast, leaf-shaped plinth of rock, the central tower rose in a diamond formation to knife-edge parapets and sheer faces. Amidst the lesser peaks, rising high above the mighty crown, the uttermost pinnacle soared to its tapered summit. The roof of Astrom was as slender and as unbreakable as a spearhead. Defying the sky and wrapped around by gale-blown snow, it looked down majestically over all.

Roujeark just stood and stared, perched precariously where he was. Cramming themselves into any nook available, his companions came and did likewise. Each one gasped as the view greeted their weary eyes. Curillian perched precariously on a rock, utterly transfixed by the sight.

'More beautiful than I dreamed…' he murmured to himself. Here it was, the object of all their toil. A new fire was kindled in each of their flagging hearts. Finally they could see, if not yet reach, their destination.

'Behold, my friends,' declared Roujeark. 'There lies Oron Amular.'

VII

An Ancient Landscape

DAYS Were running short, so they hurried along. They had been buoyed by their first view of the Mountain, but even now that it was periodically visible, it proved exceedingly slow and difficult to approach. Curillian had been counting the days off as notches on his mountain-staff, but now the skies above cleared at night and he took his reckoning from the moon again.

'We must make haste,' he urged them repeatedly. 'The moon is waxing to its full, here on the threshold of summer. The Tournament will begin soon. We must not miss the start and gift a lead to our rivals.'

Roujeark was happy to oblige, but a strange experience gave him pause one day. They were now more or less constantly in view of the Mountain, and today they were following a crude path that wound around sharp rocky bends as the crooked hills slowly descended towards the lowlands again. Suddenly he paused, the hairs on the back of his neck bristling. What was familiar about this place? The others were kept waiting behind him as he cast about in his mind. It was not until he approached the strange, flat-topped rock in a dark recess that he realised what this place was. Running his hands over the smooth rock, he remembered an old wizard sitting there. This was where he had met Kulothiel, though he had not known him at the time. In this very spot, he thought he had reached his journey's end, but in this very spot, he had been turned back. Forty years had passed between that day and this. Tears welled in his eyes as he realised that the long detour was finally over. At last, he would step closer to the Mountain. This time he would go on and reach it.

Oron Amular stood apart from the rest of the mountains, sat upon a bastion thrust out from the northern face of the range. Despite being so tall, it was exceedingly difficult to catch sight of because the mountainous approaches to south, east and west were so broken, rarely affording a clear view. Indeed, the tallest ridges to the south of the great peak were also the nearest to it, so for a long time they blocked the view of anyone coming from the east, as Roujeark and his companions were. Only from the north was there a clear view of Oron Amular, a direction well-guarded by the most secretive part of the elven realm and by the wooded fastnesses of Therenmar, the wood-elf domain.

The Mountain stood at the head of a great twin valley, where the rivers Varell and Amulir began their journeys. At first the two rivers were separated only by a long crooked ridge, but leagues and leagues downstream they separated, one skirting round the western fringe of Therenmar, and the other plunging straight through it, before they both emptied into the Troizon Ocean on Kalimar's northern coast. The Amulir was *the* river of the Mountain, issuing from right under its feet. That provenance, together with its long slow passage of the mysterious Therenmar, gave it a perilous reputation, hence its name: the Magic Water. Between Therenmar and Oron Amular, the twin valleys were practically empty of folk, the first habitations being many miles downstream. Jealously guarded of old by the League of Wizardry, even the elves had long learnt to give Oron Amular a wide berth. Therefore, the Mountain presided over a silent and untamed country.

All this they could see clearly now, but each passing day brought the prospect into sharper focus. From further off, the Mountain had seemed completely isolated and cut off from all other features, but the nearer they got, the more they realised that was simply because its sheer size dwarfed what lay about its feet. Far from being flat, the terrain about the Mountain was full of tangled forests, sharp hills and deep cloven vales, making even the northern approaches difficult. Yet all around the Mountain, immediately about its steeply-sloping feet, was a looping trough like a ditch around a fort. Tucked between mountainous slopes, it was the Mountain's own little garden.

Passing around the precipitous southern spur of the Mountain, they made their final descent into the trough, reaching its flat grassy floor in the middle of the day. They were now right underneath the Mountain, utterly dwarfed by its looming bulk. They craned their necks upwards in awe to see its lofty turrets and ice-clad flanks glittering in the sun. It was Antaya who found words to express what they were all feeling.

'This is a place Prélan paid special attention to in His work of creation. There can't be a more wondrous place in all the world, or more fearsome.'

Having arrived at last, none of them had any clear idea what to do next. They scanned the vast mountainsides, more formidable than any hand-built bastion, but no entrance or sign of life could they see.

'Well,' said Curillian, leaning on his staff, 'our great journey is at an end. We made it. But what comes next, I fear, will prove much harder.' That thought hung in the air between them before Andil asked the obvious question.

'What way in did you use when you came here before, Roujeark?'

'I fear I never actually came this far,' Roujeark answered him. 'I only came within sight of the Mountain before I was turned back.

There must be a door somewhere, but I don't know where it is.' The armists with him looked disconsolate at this revelation, but they held their peace. For want of a better plan, they followed the trough northward to see what they could find.

'It would take us days and days to walk around the whole Mountain,' said Curillian. 'I hope we get a clue before it comes to that.'

The trough was only a quarter of a mile wide, and the slopes that hemmed it in on either side were dizzyingly steep. They all felt uneasy, being trapped in such a narrow place and confronted with such formidable works of nature. The afternoon passed as they walked and they were soon cast in shade, whilst the sunlight swiftly retreated up the side of Oron Amular like a golden curtain being drawn up. When dusk fell, they settled down in a camp. As Aleinus and Caréysin prepared a meal, the stars gradually came out overhead. Being lower in altitude than they had been for some time, the guards settled down to enjoy the balmy night, but they didn't rest easy. They felt something was strange in the air here, a foreboding presence. They looked around anxiously, fearing that in every wisp of mist they might see a ghost stalking the ancient landscape.

If Curillian felt the same, he hid it well. Swathed in his cloak, he kept a patient watch, waiting for the moon to rise over the Mountain. He had waited half the night, refusing all attempts to relieve him, before the moon finally appeared over a sharp spur of ice and rock. Excitedly, he shook Roujeark awake to inspect it with him.

'Three days off full, I'd say,' judged Roujeark.

'Close enough,' agreed Curillian. 'We're early. For so long I worried we'd be late, having to come so far, but Prélan has blessed our journey.' He fell silent, regarding the luminous orb. 'I don't know what Kulothiel has planned,' mused the king, 'but whatever it is, my guess is that it will start on the day of the full moon itself, and probably at nightfall. We'd best be ready, but there's nothing we can do now except watch and wait.'

A

Which is exactly what they did. After a night under the stars, the morning dawned chill and misty. They did not venture far while the visibility remained poor, but remained in camp. As with the moon during the night, so the sun took a long time to appear over the mountainside, but when it did, the mist burned swiftly away and the deep cleft was warmed. Then they continued their explorations, following many twists and bends in the trough. Everywhere they went, though, the heavy, watchful atmosphere followed them. Not a soul did they see all day, and they were beginning to wonder whether there was a Tournament at all; or, if there was, whether anyone else would come. They were about to make another camp as evening fell when Lancoir, who was taking his turn as scout, called back to his companions.

'A light,' he informed them tersely when they came running up. 'Away there in the distance.' As they watched, the light came again, flickering like sparks being struck. Suddenly the flame caught in a fire of some sort, but it was immediately screened so that all they could make out was a faint glow.

'A campfire,' said Caréysin, who had the sharpest eyes among them.

'It would seem we're not alone in this valley after all,' said Curillian.

'Are they friends or foes, do you think?' asked Findor.

'Unless they are sentinels appointed by the Keeper, they can only be here to compete,' answered Curillian. 'I do not think Kulothiel will have invited any who might be thought of as enemies, only rivals. Come, let us go and find out who they are.'

They advanced cautiously, taking care not to be seen until they were as close as possible. Caréysin's judgement of a campfire proved correct as they drew near, but whomever it belonged to was wary, for they had taken precautions to shield it as much as possible. Night was now thick about them. Coming closer, they saw that it was a fair-sized camp: not a large gathering, but home to a larger party than their own. The owners of the fire had made their camp upon a grassy knoll rising out of the trough's bottom. Looking up from below and a little distance off, the armists inspected it as best they could. Many figures could be seen milling about, but all of them had cloaks and hoods concealing any tell-tale signs.

'It doesn't look to be a welcoming party to me,' observed Aleinus.

'There seem to be a dozen and a half or so of them, Sire,' murmured Antaya, 'but I see no banners or devices by which we might know them.'

'Sensible to stay anonymous while in a strange land,' muttered Lancoir softly.

'They are men,' declared Curillian. 'That's clear enough. But of what nation? Too discrete to be Hendarian, and too large a company to be Ciricien, I'd say. If they're from Aranar, then I may well know them. I mean to find out.'

Tiring of skulking and peering from a distance, the king straightened up and walked forward. Either the sentries were dozing, or they were looking the other way, but Curillian got quite close before they spotted him and then suddenly the whole camp was astir. A pair of figures advanced, swords drawn, but Curillian stood his ground.

'Who goes there?' shouted one, in the Common Speech. 'Declare yourself!'

Curillian strode forward another two paces and then halted on the edge of the firelight. From the challenger's voice alone, he knew that they were men of Aranar, and he chose not to speak, waiting for them to realise who he was. Unnerved by his silence, the sentries edged forward, trying to see his face.

'Who are...' the second question was cut off when a torch was brought closer and Curillian's face came fully into view.

'King Curillian,' said the other, in a wondering voice. There were two men facing him. The one who had first challenged him was tall and clad as a man-at-arms. He had not recognised Curillian, though the signs were there to see: bright hauberk of mail under a tunic embroidered with the Harolin arms, regal cloak, the great Sword of Maristonia. The other was short and stocky, better dressed, in knightly attire, and he needed no signs to recognise the armist before him. He bowed respectfully, in Aranese fashion. Curillian knew him. He was looking at Sir Hardos, Clan Knight of the Pegasus Clan, a comrade and ally of times gone by. And if Hardos was here, then his master, the Pegasus Lord, would also be present. Sure enough, a large, dark figure loomed towards them from the fire, accompanied by several others.

'Hardos, who is it?' The deep booming voice of Southilar, Jeantar of Aranar, was unmistakeable.

'An old friend, lord, sprung from the shadows.'

'Is that so? Well, let us see who our nocturnal visitor is.' As he was speaking, Southilar came into the torchlight. He was a great bear of a man, tall and broad as a gatehouse and muscled like a champion wrestler. He stood six inches taller than Curillian, and much broader. His close-cropped hair was black, though his small, neat beard was salted with grey. His dark suspicious eyes took a moment to take Curillian in.

'An old friend indeed,' said he, with barely a hint of emotion. 'No wizard's phantom this.' Then his forbidding exterior broke into a broad grin and he enveloped Curillian in a crushing bear hug, effusing as he did so.

'Curillian the Renowned, no less! And there I was thinking it was a bandit or a prowler of the night. Have you come all the way from Mariston? Great stallions! It makes me feel young again to be near you, you old campaigner!' Eventually he released Curillian and stepped back again.

'Gentlemen,' he said loudly to the men standing by, 'I give you Curillian Harolin, son of Mirkan, fabled King of Maristonia. Curillian, you may not know these milksops, for they were still slurping at their mothers' teats when last we went to war together. Here you have the baggage that no Pegasus Jeantar can do without – Clan Knights of the other clans: Lindal of the Unicorn, Deàreg of the Falcon, Acil of the Hawk and Romanthony of the Eagle.'

Next to Southilar, who was in rough garments that made him look like a travelling blacksmith, the Clan Knights were richly dressed in brocades and velvet, their weapons glittering with gems and their mail studded with ornate roundels. He did not know any of them, but he could tell their clans from the heraldic insignia each one sported proudly, and he recognised their names, for he made it his business to know about his neighbours, however new or distant. Each one bowed in turn, correct but cold in their courtesy.

'You're not alone, surely, O King of Armists?' boomed Southilar.

'No,' replied Curillian, breaking his silence at last. 'I too have companions with me.' He half-turned, and just at that moment the other armists came up into the torchlight. Lancoir and Southilar knew each other already and grasped forearms like old soldiers, but other introductions had to be made. Southilar and his knights greeted the Royal Guards of Mariston with cool aloofness, knowing the wide gulf that existed between them, for they were the nobility of their land. Southilar smiled wolfishly and boasted.

'So, you have only one Knight of Thainen, and I have no fewer than six Clan Knights – perhaps we will be a match for you this time?'

Curillian smiled easily, unfazed, while Lancoir glared challengingly at the Aranese knights, like a wolf weighing up its prey. Southilar went on volubly. 'You the noble king, me the up-jumped horse-master, and I have a larger party than you? Seldom did your ancestors, the great kings of old, go about with so little retinue. But ever was it your wont, old friend, to keep few companions and cloak yourself in mystery. Curillian, the Adventurer-king.'

If any scorn was intended in the Jeantar's jesting, the armist king chose to ignore it. 'This may be the greatest adventure of all, Southilar,' he said, 'and one where quality may count for more than quantity.' One by one, Curillian introduced his companions. Last of all, he came to Roujeark.

'Lastly, I present Roujeark, son of Dubarnik, my guide, who is known at this Mountain.' Southilar had dismissed him with a glance, but then, realising what Curillian had said, he did a double take and looked at Roujeark with amazement.

'Get away! Do you mean to tell me, Curillian, that you've got an actual wizard in your ranks?'

'I am no wizard,' spoke up Roujeark. 'But I've come here to be trained.'

'Not a wizard yet,' warned Lancoir, 'but one in the making.' Southilar laughed a deep rumble like the rolling of barrels on wooden floors.

'Careful then, my lads,' he said to his knights. 'Don't annoy the novice. I've got a wishes-he-was wizard around here somewhere. Caiasan. Not the real thing of course, blasted nuisance of a scribbler, but useful from time to time, if truth be told. Come,' he beckoned the armists. 'Come and share a flagon of ale around the fire.'

The armists followed their burly host through a makeshift camp of tents, baggage and picketed horses. They were nearing the central fire, which was well screened with tents, when a tall, dark figure stepped into Southilar's path. The shadowy figure was even taller than the Jeantar, and slim as a sword-blade next to his muscled bulk. He spoke with an elegant voice, much more cultured than the other men of Aranar.

'My lord, if it please you, I would meet the armist king.' Southilar hesitated and looked annoyed, but then stepped aside to let him through.

'Curillian, it would seem that Sir Theonar wants to make your acquaintance.' Roujeark felt a chill of foreboding as he stared up at the tall, mysterious figure, whose face was hidden by a deep hood. After a moment or two, in which he seemed to be studying the king, the tall knight went to one knee in a fluid motion and swept back his hood.

'Lord King,' he said, 'it is my deepest honour to meet you. Long have I prayed that Prélan would bring our paths together.'

The mellifluous words seemed to weave a spell before their eyes. Even Curillian, who stood barely taller than the kneeling man, seemed affected by it, regarding the knight with wonder. Wonder, too, was in Roujeark's eyes, for never had he beheld a man or armist so beautiful. He was clean-shaven, smooth-skinned and possessed of striking eyes, but it was the way that his face seemed to *shine* that really smote the beholder.

'Sir Theonar, is it?' asked Curillian, emerging swiftly from the spell. The knight nodded. 'How is it that we have not met before; you seem older than you appear?'

'Lord King, I have only had the honour of serving my lord of Pegasus for a little while.'

Southilar butted in to say more. 'If you call twenty years a little while. He's been by my side all the time I've been Jeantar, sometimes a help, sometimes a hindrance. He, Hardos, and the others helped me as I wrested the sceptre back from the other clans. 'Twas many years ere I first triumphed at Hamid that we met. My predecessor, Celkenoré, snatched him from the Unicorn Clan, which was little to their liking.'

Theonar, who had been on one knee all the while, now got up, saying as he did so, 'It is not unheard of for a common knight to transfer between clans,' he said humbly.

'Though, from what I've seen,' remarked Curillian, clearly curious, 'it is only for a rare talent that a Clan Lord will risk the controversy.'

'You are generous to suggest thus, Lord King, but I claim no such ability for myself. Lord Celkenoré saw some use in me, brought me to Hamid, and made me a Pegasus, for which I am grateful.'

'Had you always been a Unicorn prior to that?' asked Curillian. Again, Southilar interrupted.

'The horned-horse was always vague about where they found him, and neither I nor anyone I knew had seen him long on the tourney circuit.'

'The tale of my former years is, I fear, a dull one.' Roujeark watched the man's eyes flicker as he said those words, and knew them for a lie.

'Humph,' snorted Southilar. 'Wherever he came from, he came a faster swordsman and a finer horseman than he had any right to be. It's come in useful at times, I'll not deny,' he said grudgingly, 'and now he's a Clan Knight. It's a good job he doesn't yet compete in all the events, else I'd have my hands full, or more so than they are already…'

One of the other Clan Knights distracted Southilar then, and they retired to the fire together.

'Sounds like you're a good man to have around at an event like this,' said Curillian after they'd gone, looking up at the tall knight. 'We'll need to watch our step. Outside we're all friends, but inside we'll be competing against each other.' Theonar smiled deprecatingly.

'The Tournament may not be as clear-cut as that,' he said. 'My heart tells me that not all will compete alike.'

'You will compete for *the* prize, though, surely?' blurted out Roujeark. '*Power Unimaginable*?' Theonar turned to gaze at him, and held him with his eyes for an unnervingly long time.

'To each his own prize, friend. That which I seek is elsewhere.' A faraway look came into his eyes as he finally released Roujeark, and he left his last remarks unexplained. Turning back to Curillian, he said courteously, 'I hope you and I can find some time together, Lord King, before Kulothiel beckons us inside.' He nodded briefly in the direction of the looming mountain. 'There is much and more that I would know of you.'

'Then let us make a start around the fire,' said Curillian, striding in that direction. 'Have you any wine?'

Lancoir approached the king's elbow, but Curillian, taking his meaning straightaway, waved him down and made him wait. Soon they all settled down around the merry blaze, together with all those knights and men-at-arms who were not standing sentry. Apart from Curillian and Lancoir, who sat with Theonar, the armists sat together and the Aranese for the most part left them be, but one figure came to stand over them. Roujeark looked up to see a languid man with unruly hair who was chewing roasted meat from a spit with one hand

and clasping a jug of wine in the other. If his scruffy bookish clothes had not been matched by a short byrnie and dagger-belt, Roujeark might have taken him for a clerk. The smooth-cheeked newcomer stood regarding them for a few moments, swaying slightly as he did so, and then plonked himself down beside them, just before he fell over.

'So you're armists, are you?' he asked to no one in particular, although he was facing Roujeark more than the others. The direct question was good-natured, if a little slurred.

'We are,' said Antaya, annoyance grating in his tone.

'Splendid.' The man took a swig from his jug. He happened to have seated himself between Roujeark and Lionenn, and he did his best to ignore the hostility that was radiating off Lionenn like a second campfire. The Konenaire's expression left no doubt that he did not suffer fools gladly, but the genial man was undeterred. 'Never met an armist before. Seems they're just as tough, but less ugly than rumour makes them.' He smiled winningly around at all of them. Finding a mixed reception of smiles and frowns, he settled on Roujeark. 'Here, you look like my kind of chap; I'll talk to you, if you don't mind?'

Bemused by his new companion, Roujeark could only smile and nod his assent.

'Half a moment,' announced the man. 'Hold this.' He gave Roujeark custody of his jug while he finished the last chunk of meat on his skewer, which he then cast into the fire. Wiping grease on his sleeve, he took the jug back and swilled the morsel down.

'Friend, have you had any beef or wine? Come, there should still be some to go round, and for your companions too, to silence their bellies and loosen their tongues. That's the thing, for all the discomforts of the field, at least when you're on the road with the Falcon and the Hawk you're well-provisioned.' He went to collect some food, hailing

Sir Deàreg and Sir Acil as he did so, who both glanced up from their conversations to nod coolly in acknowledgement. He returned laden with more spits and clutching some cups, which he duly handed round to the armists, spilling much wine and grease in the process.

'I say, lads,' he said, surveying them seriously, 'I've brought the tuck, and the wine too. Don't s'pose you brought the women? I hear armist women are much better looking than the chaps, but just as tough, eh?' He raised his jug and toasted all of armist womanhood, seemingly. 'None to be found? Just my luck, privations of the camp and all that. No flipping fillies, ah well.'

'Our women would be too much of a handful for you, friend,' Andil told him.

'Caiasan's the name, old scout, schooling's the game. And don't worry, the more of a handful the better I say. So,' he raised his voice to proclaim, 'here's to women who are too much for us.'

Aleinus alone cheered his toast, and then promptly declared the wine to be excellent stuff.

'Proper Redmar stuff, this,' Caiasan told him. 'Some of these philistines insist on swigging beer, but just 'cos you're in the field doesn't mean you have to let standards slip, right?' Shortly after this statement, Aleinus got talking to a man-at-arms on his other side, drawing Andil and Caréysin with him. Findor and Antaya, repelled by Caiasan's conversation, fell to speaking amongst themselves, and Lionenn just sat glowering.

'Cor, he doesn't say much, does he?' Caiasan said, nodding toward the Konenaire. 'Looks like it's just us then, old lad,' he told Roujeark winningly. 'Probably for the best.' All of a sudden, he became more serious. 'Seems to me that you stand out amongst your lot no less than I do amongst mine; do we pursue similar professions?'

'I am not yet a scholar,' said Roujeark, 'but I hope to be one soon.' He let his gaze wander unwittingly to the great bulk of the Mountain, shimmering in the starlight.

'Here?' Caiasan paused mid-bite, half-choking, to ask the question in surprise. Then he let out a long soft whistle of admiration when Roujeark nodded.

'Strewth, this place is a bit beyond the likes of me. I've devoted a great part of my adult life to finding out about Oron Amular and other antiquities, but I never knew they were still admitting novices.'

'I fear I know nothing about the Mountain that would satisfy your curiosity. With his dying breath, my father sent me here forty years ago, but I was turned away with a promise that I would be able to return one day. Now, maybe, that day draws near.' Caiasan watched the far-off look smouldering in the armist's eyes. He saw too how his hands seemed to glow briefly with an inner fire when the Mountain was mentioned, even though the armist himself didn't seem to notice.

'Blimey, this is real life for you, isn't it? I mean, you're here for a real reason, not this silly Tournament?' Roujeark looked at him, surprised.

'You think it's silly to compete for *Power Unimaginable*?'

'Too bloomin' right,' Caiasan affirmed, with another swig of wine. Wiping his mouth with the back of his hand, he leaned conspiratorially close. 'Listen, friend, with some of the chaps as are here I don't think the likes of me will get much of a look in. No, they'll fight this one out between themselves, and whatever other champions turn up. And they're welcome to it. It may be that all my studies haven't turned up much, or then again, maybe they have, but I reckon whoever wins will find they've bitten off more than they can chew. Settle for scraps, I will. I mean, it's Oron Amular. You must have an idea. Think what secrets and lost knowledge lie within that Mountain. Even a fleeting peek at some of them would make my reputation. Blasted nuisance of a scribbler indeed,' he snorted indignantly, evidently well acquainted with Southilar's opinion of him. 'I'd like to put pay to remarks like that, and mayhap get one over on my peers. No more "yes, Caiasan, well done Caiasan, but now go and muck out the stables", and no more "back to your fairy-tales and fancies Caiasan, leave the real business to us". If I get out of here, I intend to be much more of a somebody when I get me back to Hamid.'

The more he drank, the more Caiasan seemed happy to chatter on about himself. And Roujeark, glad to have the attention deflected away from himself, was content to let him.

'Truth is, friend Roujeark, I'm little more than the jester on this little outing. The high 'n' mighty Jeantar's pet. You'd think they treat me better, seeing as how I got 'em here, not to mention cleaning up their cuts and scrapes along the way. Unappreciated, that's my trouble.' He sniffed loudly, and wiped a sleeve across his nose.

'You guided your party here?' Roujeark asked, thinking he was not quite as unique as he thought. Slowly, the rambling truth came out, meandering ever more so as the wine claimed the scribe's wits.

'Yes…well, mostly. Knew vaguely where the Mountain might be, but got a little stuck after the High Falls. Good job that chieftain from, whaddya call it, Ilk, 'at's it, turned up. Never seen such a strange chap, but he set us right for a while…then we ran into that older blighter, claimed 'e was from old Ithilia, flipping fibber. Anyhow, he led us a right merry dance through most of eastern Dorzand before one day he just vanished in the fog.' By now, Caiasan was practically lying in Roujeark's lap, having started off slouching against him. Still cradling his wine jug, and talking more to himself than to the armist, he carried on, fending off sleep and discoursing blearily on.

'Oh, how we struggled in that accursed waste of rock and bog. Day after day, never getting anywhere. Food running short.' He interrupted himself with a loud belch. 'We would have been in a real tight spot had we not been spotted by the elf border-guards. Least, think tha's what t'were. They took pity on us, remembering kindly some good turn or other that our ancestors did 'em back in the Second War. 'Gainst the rules they packed us down some steep valley, and then, flip, we were in Kalimar…avoided the towns and cities… crossed the rivers quiet-like…eventually wound up here. Fine service I rendered.' Another belch, this one less volcanic. 'And how was I rewarded? With…with…' he raised his jug feebly for another sip, but it never made it to his lips, as he finally fell asleep.

A

Curillian smiled when he saw the Aranese scribe slumped in sleep against Roujeark. The young wizard was trapped and couldn't get up, but he seemed close to sleep himself. Half the camp was drifting back to their tents by now, and the sentries were being changed. Judging this as good a moment as any, Curillian had Findor and the others pitch their own shelters in the Aranese camp, and then he slipped off with Lancoir. They made their way to a smaller knoll some way from the larger one, and stood talking, out of earshot of the camp.

'A jolly evening,' Lancoir said mirthlessly. He looked bored and restless.

'You mean you weren't riveted by the endless tales of prowess with which we were regaled?' Lancoir scowled for answer. 'Yes, brave and reliable they may be, but the men of Aranar can be more than a little brash. Count yourself lucky if you can ever get them to talk about more than horses, tourneys and ale.' In truth, Curillian had found the evening just as tedious as Lancoir, having been ignored by Southilar for most of the time and left to converse with small-minded Pegasus knights.

'That Sir Theonar seemed a bit different,' remarked Lancoir.

'Yes, but he wasn't there for long. I didn't see when he slipped off.'

'He retired quietly when Southilar started on his third tankard. Just melted into the night.' Curillian smiled.

'A pity,' said the king. 'His conversation would probably have been more engaging than what I ended up getting. I didn't get much of the Jeantar's time. Truth be told, he seemed far more interested in the company of the Hawk and the Falcon.'

'I noticed that too. Strange bedfellows.'

Curillian smiled. 'Not much gets past you eh, Lancoir?'

'Except me, just now,' said a new voice.

Curillian and Lancoir both whirled around, swords in hand instantaneously. For a moment, they could see nothing, but they could hear the heavy breathing. Then the darkness of night thickened into a deeper shade. Slowly, an old, unsteady figure shuffled out of the darkness, leaning heavily on a curious staff. Lancoir stepped in front of his king, brandishing his sword in a defensive stance.

'Aye, but I've marked you now. Who are you?'

Curillian laid a soothing hand on Lancoir's arm. 'Not so loud, Lancoir, maybe our visitor doesn't want to alert the whole camp.' Slowly he felt the tension in the knight's arm relax, and then he straightened into a more relaxed posture.

'Might we know who you are, sir, and why you sneak up on us in the dark?' The figure kept shuffling forward, nearer to them, and he seemed to be making an odd sound, like an old man chuckling softly to himself.

'An old man has little other option for approaching folk in the night when he has no light. As for who I am, my name would not do you much good I'm afraid – it is very difficult to pronounce.'

'Still, a name would be a comfort,' said Curillian. 'An honest name, however difficult to pronounce, would make the wise man feel better about his unbidden night-time guest.' Again, the chuckling sound came, but still the old man had not raised his head enough for them to see under his hood.

'Fairly said, but you are an armist, not a man. Even more fair is for the stranger to declare himself first, for I am more at home here than you, I think. I was curious to see who would be first. But an old man has to be wise too, you see, in times when folk lie, cheat and steal to come to the Mountain that was lost.'

Curillian bridled. 'We did not lie, cheat or steal to come hither. Ours is a noble motive, and honest have been our steps.'

'*Indeed*, is that so?' said the stranger. 'Then you are singularly set apart from many who draw nigh. Invites they may have to the Tournament in yonder mountain, but that does not mean that their conduct in the approach will go unmarked. Pride, greed, envy, lust – do these sound to you like traits that will be rewarded?'

'Sir,' countered Curillian, 'you seem to know a lot about what passes in the hearts of contestants who are not even here yet. How may that be?'

'Do you not know that those who walk in this land have many ways of knowing things? Secrets stay less easily buried in these vales. Come, I bid you, can you declare that you come here for reasons other than those I have named?' The voice was undoubtedly that of an old man, but it had grown in power since the first soft words.

'I come to see what else my life may yet hold in store,' declared Curillian. 'I live and compete in the name of Prélan, the living God.' The old man raised his head a fraction at these words, enough for them to see a jut of chin, and the glimmer of eyes hidden deep in the hood's recesses.

'And what would be the hallmarks of a contestant thus conducted?' The question and queer glance together chilled Curillian's heart, though he could not think why, for he spoke in good faith. The virtues rattled off his tongue almost before he was aware of them.

'Courage, steadfastness, humility, temperance, mercy, clemency.'

The old man nodded along as the words came. Then he swept back his hood. For a split second, he loomed large, eyes blazing, and then he seemed to vanish in a gust of wind. Curillian and Lancoir turned away, shielding their faces with their arms as the chill draught flowed over them. But the single word uttered could not be warded off, and Curillian heard it within his head and without, penetrative and lingering.

Remember...

A

Roujeark sat alone on the edge of the camp. Having finally extricated himself from the slumbering Caiasan, he had settled down to gaze at the Mountain, dark beneath, and luminescent above. The more he gazed, the more he seemed to lose himself in the otherworldly sight. The air seemed to grow warmer and a strange breeze wafted up. Then suddenly he heard hot words within his head.

'Are you ready to begin? Is this truly the path you wish for yourself? Will you be ready to leave them all?'

VIII
The Contestants Convene

The next morning dawned upon a somewhat dishevelled camp, one which slowly came to life as the last sentries and duty cooks were joined by knights and men-at-arms waking tender-headed. On stools around the breakfast fire, Curillian and the armists found themselves joined by Sir Theonar. As they ate their bowls of porridge, talk inevitably fell to the Tournament.

'Still not much sign of anything happening on the Mountain,' remarked Aleinus. 'How long will we just sit here?'

'Last night the moon was still two days off the full,' said Roujeark. 'That means it isn't due to start until tomorrow night.'

'Fear not, Aleinus,' said Curillian. 'I shouldn't expect much to happen before more competitors are here. We are the only ones at present, but my guess is that others will arrive today.'

As they talked, others came and joined them, including an unshaven Caiasan, looking much the worse for wear. The conversation widened, and as it did so, Curillian and Theonar began talking between themselves.

Lancoir was too disciplined a soldier to remain idle for long, so as soon as he'd devoured his porridge he abandoned his bowl and walked the circuit of their camp. Their situation was not as defensible as he would have liked, but the position atop the knoll was better than anything else in prospect. He finished his circuit on the west brow of the knoll and joined one of the Aranese sentries, a Pegasus man-at-arms whose stomach was growling.

'Go get some food,' Lancoir told the man. 'I'll keep watch.' He looked out west in the dim morning light created by the Mountain's shadow. The sentry had not gotten far before Lancoir recalled him. 'No, wait!' Despite owing no obedience to this armist, the man-at-arms scurried back, curious as to what had alerted his new companion. For a long time Lancoir didn't say anything else, but stood straining his eyes against the half-light. Before them was the widest stretch of the trough they had yet come across, where there was quite a gap between the mountainside and the opposite slopes. In that wide space the mists were already mostly lifted, but beyond, where a great spur of the Mountain reached out almost to within touching distance of the cloven trough's far side, fog still lay heavy in the narrow place.

'There,' said Lancoir, now more confident of his sighting. 'Yes, there. See, figures moving through the mist.' The sentry strained his eyes thither as well, but by the time he had even located them, Lancoir had counted their number. 'Seven. Men on foot.' He turned to the sentry. 'Go give word to His Majesty the King, tell him there are new arrivals. Ask him to join me here.'

Others heard these words, and so a small crowd had gathered by the time Curillian came up with the armists and Theonar in tow. Lancoir pointed out the distant movement to his king.

'There, sire, men moving in the mist. Seven of them. I think they may be men of Ciricen.'

'Yes, they come from Ciricen,' pronounced Theonar. 'See how dull and sombre their apparel is, all grey mail, dark fur and hardened leather? They move with the accustomed caution of their race, and

172

come well-armed. They each bear a skux, the axe-like weapon that only the Lordai wear, as well as more besides…'

Curillian smiled, marvelling. 'You are far-sighted, friend; I cannot see any of that.'

'Believe him, lord king,' piped up one of the Pegasus men. 'Sir Theonar has the best eyes I know.'

Gradually the newcomers came on, and slowly the distinctive characteristics of their garb and gear that had been apparent long before to Theonar became visible to the others. Around the same time, the small company halted, seemingly now aware that their approach was being watched. After a short while they came on again, their caution redoubled. In the time they took to draw near, Curillian was able to answer some questions posed to him by those around him.

'Who are the Lordai, Curillian?' asked Roujeark. 'Are they the same as the men of Ciricen?' To Roujeark, growing up in one of Maristonia's high valleys, Ciricen was just the name of a distant land, its people little more than a vague rumour beyond the edge of firm knowledge.

'No, Roujeark, Ciriciens and Lordai are not necessarily the same, for although the Lordai are a clan only found in Ciricen, not every man of Ciricen is reckoned to be a Lordul. The distinction is centuries old, coming from a time when the character of the men of Ciricen began to greatly diverge, between those remained noble on the one hand and those who fell into darkness on the other. The Lordai were those who retained their dignity, named for their first chieftain. They opposed the Sordai, who forsook the lore and traditions of their forebears and conspired with the Northmen for their own profit. Ever after Ciricen was a realm divided, doomed to endure long ages of evil and chaos that culminated in the Second War of Kurundar, when I was young. After bitter struggle, the Lordai emerged victorious to reclaim the throne of Ciricen, but they had become a grim folk, iron-hard and dour.' All were listening with great fascination, for such lore was not commonly known, in Aranar or in Maristonia. Findor asked another question.

'Sire, that is ancient history and long ago. What do you know of these men and their purposes today?'

'Thónarion sits on the throne in Rohandur today, Findor, as you should know well. He is beset by war and sedition, both of which arose again to trouble Ciricen in the time of his father, Liotor, but a little while after the royal authority had been restored. Bleak is his outlook, with the return of the Sordai and the rebuilding of Haracost. So much, at least, my Royal Guards should know,' said Curillian, with gentle reproof. 'As for what their purposes are, that is harder to say.'

'If I may speak, lord king,' said Sir Theonar respectfully, 'I am surprised that men of Ciricen have come hither at all. They are too much occupied with their own troubles, or so I deemed. But since some have indeed come, perhaps one of the Lordai has it in mind to win a weapon of great power. Now that the fell city of Haracost has been rebuilt, his kin are in desperate need of some such aid if they are to prevail again over their ancient enemies.'

No one knew how Theonar came by such knowledge, which was hardly common, even amongst the great lords of Aranar, but few of his countrymen at hand seemed surprised. Curillian was surprised, and marked it, but he was also in agreement. While they had been speaking, the men had drawn near. One of their number, a huge man, stepped forth and held his weapon aloft, haft-first in gesture of peace. It was a curious weapon, somewhere between a short halberd and a throwing axe, single-bladed but surmounted by a vicious-looking spike. This, and many other strange things about the Ciriciens, could be discerned as they came closer, but nothing that looked rich or princely.

Responding to the big man's gesture, Curillian went partway down the knoll's slope to meet them with Lancoir at his side. Since Southilar was nowhere to be seen, Sir Theonar went to represent Aranar, and with him went Lindal, the supercilious Unicorn Clan-knight. The whole Ciricien party came forward, but five of them hung back slightly. The big man who had waved the skux led the way, another close behind him.

'Hail, men of Ciricen,' spoke Curillian loudly. 'Unless you mean to start the Tournament prematurely, then come in peace and be welcome in this place of waiting.' The big man, with scarred face and hard eyes, looked Curillian up and down, but gave no answer. Instead, his companion stepped forward. He was a smaller man, but stern and well-built all the same.

'I am not a man of lore, but even one from far Centaur knows that only Curillian of Mariston could speak thus. Did ever an armist live so long and yet look so young? And if I guessed not from your bearing, I know the Sword of Maristonia by your side truly enough, of which we have heard, but not seen, in my country.'

Curillian bowed stiffly. 'Is it the earl of Centaur that I speak to, Culdon, of formidable repute?'

The man slammed a fist into his armoured chest by way of salute. 'I am he, and here with me is Garthan, my master-at-arms, and five others of my household. But I see men of Aranar beside you, King Curillian, and not armists only. Do we look to compete against you together, or severally?' Theonar gave answer for his people.

'My lord of Centaur, you find the two here together by happy chance, not conspired design. Oft have armists and the men of Aranar stood side by side as allies in war, so do not be surprised to find evidence of friendship between them. Yet you need not worry, both now welcome you, and both will compete against you in their own right if you mean to enter the Tournament.'

Earl Culdon came forward then, and scarce could he have looked less like an earl in the eyes of Roujeark. In his small experience, the great lords of Maristonia were far grander in their appearance than this grim, simply clad warrior. But he was relieved to see the newcomer accepted in friendship by the king and Sir Theonar. Coming closer, he heard the other members of the Ciricien company named.

'Anrhus, my scout…and these here are warriors of my household: Rufin, Narheyn, Rhyard and Kaspain.' Each looked as severe and doughty as the last. All were armoured in leather and mail beneath their cloaks and furs, and armed to the teeth with swords, daggers, hunting spears and skuxs. The first three, who were all dark-haired, bore three faded chevrons on hardened-leather surcoats, while blond Kaspain, the last-named and youngest-looking, had only one. Roujeark missed some of what was said, but one thing he heard was very interesting, although it made him nervous.

'We are not the only ones who will arrive to disturb you today,' Culdon told Curillian. 'We have travelled far now in company with the Hendarian host, though at the last we tired of their slow pace and came on ahead. I think they were happy to let us do the scouting.'

The men of Ciricen set to making a small bivouac for themselves a little apart from the existing encampment. As they did so, Lancoir seized Curillian's elbow and hissed urgently in his ear.

'A host of Hendarians? We are too few if they decide to make trouble…'

'I don't think you need worry, Lancoir. How large a host can they have sent on such a road? If King Idunar is too old to give thought to this Tournament, then doubtless one of his brothers will have sent a champion with a suitable escort, but I do not think they will be many. Besides, competitors will need more than numbers to win this Tournament. If these Hendarians think they can bully through with sheer weight of men, then they have sorely misjudged Kulothiel's mind. Still, let us be on our guard.'

A

They did not have to wait long before the next arrivals turned up. They heard them long before they saw them, because a fanfare of trumpets smote the air and set the quiet air of the mountain vale to ringing. The noise was enough to bring Southilar forth from his tent at last. Drying a newly washed face with a towel, he strode grumbling to join them.

'What cur is winding trumpets at this hour?' he demanded gruffly. 'Are we beset by an army?'

'Behold, my lord,' said Curillian. 'Hendar has arrived.'

'Trust the Hendarians to make such a racket, always showing off...' grumbled Hardos, who stood beside his master.

The sun had now risen high enough to glance off the helms and spear-points of the cavalcade that was emerging from the last of the mist. Issuing out of the narrow place, the mounted party fanned out into a broad line of horses. They seemed to be mostly clad in metal, because when they came clearly into view, they caught the sun like mirrors and dazzled from afar. Shielding their eyes, the waiting leaders watched their onset.

'Only twenty,' breathed Theonar. 'But there was something strange about that fanfare...' His voice trailed off.

'It seems we need not have worried,' murmured Curillian to Lancoir. 'The Hendarians come with as much pomp as ever, but not so many in number as we might have expected.'

Roujeark was struck by the contrast between these men and those who had arrived before. The Hendarians were mounted, and came on arrogantly and full of confidence, where the Lordai had been on foot and so discrete as to be almost secretive. And after the nondescript drabness of Earl Culdon's party, the Hendarians were gorgeous in bright and ostentatious colours. Wealth and distinction were much in evidence as they drew nearer. After a while, the mounted group halted, and suddenly great banners were unfurled. As they caught the breeze, the brief relaxation of the waiting onlookers twitched rapidly into new anxiety, and murmurs of wonder rippled through them. Roujeark wondered why this flag had agitated them all so. He saw a great shield divided into five parts, each bearing its own token. Over all was set a crown and crossed spears, and stars twinkled in the scarlet field. Precious thread and sewn jewels made the whole device sparkle and glitter in the sun.

'The royal banner of Hendar,' said Curillian aloud. 'Has King Idunar come in person?' Southilar was incredulous.

'What? The old miser himself? Must have finally gotten sick of those squabbling brothers of his...'

'My lords,' said Sir Theonar, demurring. 'King Idunar has been wracked by illness for some time now, and hasn't been able to ride for months. This cannot be he.' Southilar ignored him, but Curillian looked troubled. By now, the Hendarian riding had started moving forwards again, coming swiftly closer.

'If this is not Idunar,' declared Curillian, 'then it can only be one other. The dukes of Malator and Nalator do not ride under the royal emblem, they would bear their own ducal arms. This can only be the

Crown Prince, Adhanor.' New murmurs greeted this identification, as men wondered what it might mean.

'Lord king,' said Theonar quietly, 'the Crown Prince has his own token. If he rides with the king's banner, surely it means that the old king is dead and a new star rises in Hendar?' These words, spoken softly enough, were caught by enough ears to cause widespread amazement and shock. The king of Hendar, dead!

'But why would the prince be here if he has a kingdom to secure?' asked Sir Romanthony. 'This would be a dangerous time to go questing.'

'The allure of Oron Amular is stronger than we thought,' remarked Curillian. 'But certainly, strange tidings are afoot.'

Soon it was beyond all doubt. Five riders broke away from the main party, and, cantering forwards, they reined in their horses at the foot of the knoll. One bore the great banner, and he that led them bore a golden circlet on his elaborate helm. No old man could ride thus. The five riders waited at the foot of the knoll, as if expecting the onlookers to come down, but eventually they tired of waiting and dismounted. All five came up, led by the crowned man who now took off his helm to reveal a shock of fair hair. The knight who struggled on foot with the great flag remained behind armour and visor, but the other riders also removed their helms. One was old and grizzled, but the other two were as young and handsome as the leader.

His face full of wonder, the leader halted and surveyed the faces above him. The older man, all in plate armour, stepped forward and announced his master in an uncompromising bark.

'Behold His Most Serene Highness, Adhanor, King of Hendar, Master of the Five Cities and Guardian of the North.' So, thought Curillian, it's true. The old king was dead, and yet his son and heir was here, hundreds of leagues away. That's inconvenient timing, for the invite to arrive just as the kingdom changes hands. This Adhanor was young, barely into full adulthood. Curillian had never met him, but already he began to guess at his character. An impulsive youth, and daring, but reckless and irresponsible.

'Strangers,' the older man barked again. 'Declare yourselves.' Only now did the leaders on the brow of the knoll come down, and none of them really looked the part. Curillian and Lancoir were road-worn and travel-stained, and Southilar was not even fully dressed yet. Only the Clan Knights Romanthony of the Eagle, Lindal of the Unicorn and Hardos and Theonar of the Pegasus bore any insignia of rank and realm. Curillian was foremost in courtesy and greeting.

'Hail Adhanor, King of Hendar, and well met. I did not know your late father the king as well as I would have liked, but I am glad to meet you so early in your reign.' Adhanor looked searchingly at Curillian, as if trying to place him, and then seemed to arrive at an answer.

'Curillian? Curillian of Mariston?'

The armist nodded.

'It is you!' Adhanor gave a perfunctory bow. 'Lord King, the honour of this meeting is mine. Earl Culdon I know already, for he and his men were good enough to accompany us on the road for some time. And these,' he said, looking at the men beside Curillian, 'are surely my neighbours of Aranar, knights and princes of the horse.' He spoke with an easy gallantry, but there was conceit in his eyes, and in the eyes of his companions who looked on. 'Southilar I know, at least, the noble Jeantar, but who are these others?' Southilar grunted noncommittally, so Sir Theonar introduced himself, Hardos, Romanthony and Lindal.

'Well met, sirs,' declared Adhanor. 'And let me introduce my companions.' He gestured first to the big man in full plate armour who had announced him. 'Onandur, Count of Oloyir, Captain of my

Bodyguards and makeshift royal herald. Xavion, Count of Koros, who has grown up at my side, and my particular friend, Reubun, Duke of Lalator.' The two elegant young men stood apart, aloof, and surveyed the ragged welcome committee with cool eyes.

'Your Grace,' said Curillian, 'it is a great grief to us to hear of the passing of King Idunar. On behalf of all Maristonia, I offer you my condolences. I hope that his passing was in peace?'

'An illness took him,' Adhanor said carelessly, 'but his time was ripe.'

That's true enough, thought Curillian, for 220 years old was well-advanced even for a king of Hendar in these days, but there's more to this than the boy lets on. Rather than continue the conversation there in the open, Curillian disengaged and Adhanor returned to his horse. The rest of the Hendarian cavalcade came up, and soon their tents were sprouting like velvet mushrooms on the ground before the knoll. Curillian sought out Adhanor while his great royal pavilion was being erected around him. The young king was standing while a squire unfastened his bulky outer armour. Duke Reubun and Count Xavion were there also, seated discretely off to one side.

'Ah, my lord Curillian, good of you to come and visit me. This is Athrick, my squire. Athrick, meet the king of the armists.'

The stout teenager looked up bashfully, but could not muster a greeting. He hurriedly finished his task and withdrew from the pavilion.

'A good lad,' Adhanor told Curillian, 'but shy.' He sat back in a camp chair and sipped from a goblet of wine that Athrick had poured earlier. Curillian declined a goblet of his own, looking around the richly decorated interior. He had something similar himself, but he rarely used it, for when on the road he either stayed in one of his estates, or with a noble host or a religious house. On ventures such as this, though, he preferred the simple trappings of an army officer. To regain his attention, Adhanor began speaking.

'So, it looks like we've got quite an international crowd already. Men of three different nations, and armists. Do you think many more will come?'

'I believe so, Your Grace. It is my understanding that invitations went out to the leaders and lords of every nation and race. We will probably see elves and even dwarves before long.'

'Dwarves?' Adhanor seemed astounded, and shared a smile with his noble attendants. 'Well, that *will* make it interesting.'

'And more men may yet come...' added Curillian.

'There will be no others from Ciricen,' announced Count Xavion from the half-shadows in the pavilion's eaves. 'Friend Culdon told us as much. He nearly didn't come himself.'

'Well,' said Curillian, 'our friends the Lordai have many concerns at the moment, some more pressing than this Tournament. Will there be any more of your own folk, Your Grace?' Curillian was not genuinely worried, but behind the casual enquiry was a faint suspicion that Hendar might be seeking to turn the situation to its own advantage. Once more, it was not Adhanor who answered, but one of his companions, Duke Reubun this time.

'No others shall come from the kingdom of Hendar,' he declared loftily. 'I have seen to it that no lord or knight rode forth without leave. All those in this riding were carefully vetted. As you can imagine, my lord, the kingdom is much astir because of recent events. Each nobleman, from the great dukes to the lowliest knight, is busy making ready for the new reign.' Curillian instinctively disliked the pompous young aristocrat, who reclined so languidly, cup of wine in hand, and he marvelled at the casual hypocrisy in the words.

'And yet, you, my lords,' he addressed the young noblemen, 'are here?' Adhanor made a deprecatory noise, sipping again from his wine.

'My uncles are taking care of everything. My crowning is not due until the end of summer, and nothing else required my immediate attention. But this, on the other hand,' he gestured vaguely out of the pavilion entrance-flap. 'How could I pass this up? You've had your fair share of adventures, my lord, or so I was taught. Surely you understand? And why else would you be here…?'

'That is true enough,' conceded Curillian. 'Though it is probably not been as romantic as your tutors may have made it out to be. I too was young when my father was taken from me, but unlike yourself, I did not have the good fortune to come straight into my own. Long years and dangerous roads I walked before ascending the throne, and those trials prepared me well for it, teaching me to value it properly.' Reubun seemed to sniff dismissively, but Curillian ignored him.

'Come, my lord,' said Adhanor, 'I hope you aren't here to lecture me? Or is it that you're afraid of a little more competition?' The young king smiled disarmingly, but his challenge was unmistakeable. Just at that moment, two other men entered the pavilion, as different as chalk and cheese. One was a small, wry-faced man, immaculate in scholarly robes, whose faint smile showed that he had heard the last exchange. The other, bulky and red-faced, stood uncomfortably by the entrance in ill-fitting royal livery. The neat little man introduced himself and the other.

'Lord King, allow me to introduce myself. I am Equerrin, Physician to His Grace, and most pleased to make your acquaintance. That sweating oaf by the door is Rothger, a sheriff of the realm, and our pathfinder.' Curillian looked at Rothger.

'You guided the king's party all the way here?' The sheriff looked uncomfortable being addressed, but his eyes were shrewd enough. They darted around, and then settled on the floor as he mumbled an answer.

'Me lord? I found paths for His Grace and their lordships as best I could, but 'twas the bishop who did it really.' Curillian nodded, and cocked an eyebrow at Adhanor, who, in turn, gestured for the physician to elaborate.

'What Rothger means is that Bishop Nurvo, an esteemed member of our expedition, has a rare knowledge of this Mountain that he was only too happy to put at the disposal of his new sovereign.'

Curillian took this information in, and then turned his attention back to Adhanor.

'You are fortunate to have such a person in your following.' Then he changed tack, curious. 'The Lords Malator and Nalator are well, I trust?' Rumoril, Duke of Malator, and Dencaril, Duke of Nalator, were the greatest magnates in Hendar, and brothers to the late King Idunar. They had dominated his reign, and Curillian wondered what sort of dynamic would reveal itself between the old tyrants and the young successor.

'They are well,' Adhanor replied. 'It is a great relief knowing I have two such experienced men of government to rely on while I am here.' He scrutinised Curillian curiously for a while, as if pondering some great question, and an uncomfortable silence grew. Curillian paused a few heartbeats and then took his leave.

'Your Grace, I am glad to see you settled. Now, if you will excuse me.' He had reached the flap and was halfway out when Adhanor called after him, voicing the question which had obviously been needling him.

'And you, my lord, how did you find your way here?' Curillian paused and then looked back over his shoulder.

'I, too, have a guide.'

Ducking out of the tent, he had only gone a few strides in the waxing morning light when he bumped into a dark-robed figure. The figure made respectful apologies and made to move on straightaway, but Curillian checked him. The man looking at him had oil-slicked hair above strong aquiline features and glimmering black eyes.

'You are the bishop who guided King Adhanor?' Curillian guessed. The man smiled modestly, but his eyes gave nothing away.

'Your Majesty is well informed. I am Nurvo, Bishop of Losantum, a lowly priest in the service of the Hendarian church.' Curillian's skin prickled and he remained alert and firm.

'Yet you know of Oron Amular?' Again, the modest smile.

'Some of my, ah, rather…unique studies have led me here, yes. If Your Majesty will excuse me, I must attend to my services…' Without a backward glance, he moved suavely on.

Curillian watched him go, and only then did he notice the other priest who shadowed the bishop, black-clad and surreptitious. After a while, a third man went by as well, another nobleman, older and pale, but whose concentration was wearily fixed on the two priests. Curillian was puzzled by the atmosphere and the peculiar body language, and he mulled over the morning's conversations on his way back to his own tent. With several parties now joined together, the camp had swelled to a small temporary village, but the different nations had separated themselves out now into distinct quarters. Lancoir waited by the armist tents.

'Lancoir,' the king said, 'strange things are going on amongst the Hendarians. It may be nothing, but see what you can find out.'

The day wore on and Curillian found some more time to talk to Sir Theonar, sitting together on the brow of the knoll facing Oron Amular. The tall knight told him many tales of his life, but all vague and unassuming. Presently they were interrupted as Adhanor came up, all brash confidence and bullish charm.

'So, when will the wizard make his move?' he called. Roujeark, who had also joined them and sat nearby, started, afraid, but then he realised that the Hendarian king had no idea who he was, and had been referring to Kulothiel. Adhanor was dressed for action. He rubbed his hands together eagerly as he surveyed the Mountain, as if expecting its hidden gates to be flung wide at any moment. He was soon distracted, though, by sounds coming down the valley. His head turned to look in that direction, and soon all eyes were turned thither also. Curillian and Theonar came to stand by the Hendarian king. A lot of noise announced the arrival of many people into the valley. Not long had passed before it became clear that several different parties were arriving at once.

Aided by Theonar's sharp sight, Curillian did his best to tell them apart. A doughty contingent of dwarves came marching into the broader part of the valley, throwing up much dust beneath their heavy boots. Iron-shod, mailed and armoured, they were a grim folk who looked ready for trouble. Behind them, and to the side, rode a large ragged group, free-riders of Aranar by the look of them. Male and female, hardened soldiers of fortune all. Hardly needing a closer look, Curillian had rarely seen such a surly and disreputable band. Unless the watchers' eyes were mistaken, there seemed to be more distinguished persons dotted amongst them, tall enough to be elves, but way-worn. Curillian could not guess what had brought together such a combination, nor where this band ended and the next began, for dozens of lordless mortals were now milling about in the confusion of the valley. Most astonishing of all, there came a crew of Alanai, barbarian men out of the south. Curillian wouldn't have believed it had anyone other than Theonar announced them. It was to them in particular that his attention was turned as the assorted newcomers gradually came closer to the camps.

'They are olive-skinned and proud of face,' Theonar told Curillian.

'That makes them sound like men of Raduthon,' Curillian guessed from the description. 'For the tribes and city-dwellers further south are darker of skin, some as dark as charcoal and ebony. Do they have curved sabres and flowing robes?'

'Yes,' said the Aranese knight. 'Their heads are covered with gem-set turbans, and scarves cover their faces up to their noses. They wear sandals and carry short bows and wicker quivers. And if my eyes do not deceive me, I believe there are both men and women in this crew, equally fierce of face and equally well-armed.'

'This is astonishing,' said Curillian. 'I know the invitations went far and wide, but I am amazed that they went as far as Lurallan. Truly, Kulothiel means this to be a varied gathering.'

'I do not know what surprises me more,' agreed Theonar. 'That they were invited at all, or that they managed to get here. Kulothiel's influence with the elves of Kalimar must still run deeper than I guessed for them to suffer such as these to pass.'

'They're savages,' spat Adhanor contemptuously. He knew the Alanai far less well than did Curillian, whose constant concern was to guard his southern frontier against them, but his prejudice was none the less keen for his ignorance. 'However they came, they will yield to better men in this tourney.'

Now, with such a blend of different races and nations present, the leaders of each group went among their followers to make pre-emptive preparations. Suspicions ran high, with many fearing and guarding against ambush. Not a few old grudges and grievances were now thrust uncomfortably close together, making for a tense atmosphere. Curillian took counsel with Lancoir and Roujeark.

'This will require great care. With so much fuel, the slightest spark could cause a conflagration. I mean to bring the various leaders together and secure a truce until the Tournament starts. Lancoir, go to the dwarf company and assure them that they are welcome and not under threat. Bid their chieftain come to our gathering, so that his kind may be represented.'

Curillian sent Antaya with a similar embassy to the Alanai. As messages went also to the other contingents, Curillian took stock with Roujeark.

'9 *Alanciel*. Last day before the full moon. It will begin tomorrow night.'

'Everyone's here now, do you think?' asked the wizard.

'It may well be, Roujeark.'

Just then, though, Curillian noticed three discrete riders passing up the valley from the other direction, whence the armists themselves had come. Tall, elegant, beautifully garbed and riding magnificent horses, they were unmistakably elves of Kalimar, and yet each as different to each other as the sea is from the plain, and the plain from the forest.

'Three kindreds, three representatives,' breathed Curillian. 'An Avatar princess and lords from the coast and from the forest.' The three riders kept well apart, and went unnoticed by most of those present, but Curillian watched as a slight scuffle broke out and three others broke away from the rudimentary camp of the free-riders to join them. His guess that elves had been among the free-riders was proved correct, but the reason for it still eluded him. Now, watching them ride across the valley, it became clear to his eyes that they were Ithrillian elves, dressed more sombrely than their Kalimari kin, and yet also distinct in other ways less easy to describe. The six took counsel briefly together on horseback, and then withdrew silently.

⋀

The gathering of the leaders was a surreal experience, like nothing Curillian had ever seen before. He had travelled far and wide, and fought beside folk of most free nations, but never had he seen so many brought together in one place and time. He looked round the bizarre circle, marvelling at the wide array of faces, garments, accoutrements, stances, and weapons. There was Southilar, Jeantar of Aranar, still dressed like a blacksmith but lordly in stature; Culdon, the dour earl of Centaur in Ciricen, grim as a guard of graves; Adhanor, King of Hendar, boisterous yet regal; Hoth, a stout dwarf-lord out of long-forgotten Carthak, proud and wary; Parthir, the Alanai captain whose dark eyes glowered above a half-hidden face, and who was flanked by two female members of his crew, faces half-hidden like his own but regarding all about them with a fierce glance; and a long-faced Aranese knight errant who named himself Sir Losathen the Luckless. Last of all there was himself, armist king of Maristonia. Curillian doubted such an assembly of lords and kings had been seen since the Great Alliance overthrew Kurundar in the First War. And yet this was just a flavour of the mix of free-folk milling about around them, where walked bishops and knights, scribes and healers, mercenaries and rogues. Quite a cast.

'My lords,' he addressed them. 'We are all here with the same purpose, and by the same invitation. Let us compete long and hard for this prize that has been set before us, but let us save our energies for the Tournament itself. There should be no enmity among us here, lest this ancient valley be filled with needless blood. Some of you I know, and some I have had dealings with in the past, but I have no quarrel with any of you.' He fixed his eyes especially here on Parthir and his attendants, the Alanai representatives, who had been so reluctant to come. Whatever lay in the past between their two peoples, there was no need for any of it here. 'We have but one more day to wait, I deem, before the Tournament begins. None of us should suffer harm before we hear the wizard speak. So, my lords, help me keep a truce until we are inside the Mountain. Let old scores be forgotten until we are inside. Help me, by each of you restraining his own folk. We shall soon all have the chance to test ourselves. When the time comes, may the greatest of us prevail, but until that time, let peace reign among us.'

After a brief clamour and argument, they all assented with varying levels of enthusiasm. Gradually, and not without some muttering and jostling, they dispersed to preach this accord to their followers. Only as the council was breaking up did Curillian notice a latecomer who had not been present at first. He recognised the tall elf, despite the new scars on his face and the rents in his armour.

'You ask more than you know, Curillian,' he said, eyes smouldering.

'Elrinde! Are you Lancearon's representative here? It's so good to see you after all these years.' This Ithrillian lord had been right-hand elf to Lancearon for many lifetimes longer than Curillian could remember. Whether as king of Ithrill, or Silver Emperor, Lancearon had relied heavily on the many talents of Elrinde, both as a warrior and a politician. Now it seemed Elrinde was resuming the role of ambassador that he had played on several previous occasions. Curillian had fought under Elrinde's command, and alongside him, for many years during the Second War of Kurundar. As a young armist, living in exile and not yet come to the height of his powers, Curillian had been trained and encouraged by the noble elven lord. He had learnt so much. Through many battles and skirmishes, he had never seen Elrinde suffer so much as a scratch, nor lose his ready smile, but the elf that stood before him now was battered and bruised. Suppressed anger radiated from him.

'I will observe your truce, Curillian, because you ask it. But there are some in this gathering who will die very quickly after they have entered the Mountain.' Curillian shivered – Elrinde did not issue idle threats – but he was mystified. He thought Elrinde must have been one of the elves who had come with the free-riders of Aranar, but who had left them immediately upon arriving at the camp to join the other elves.

'Elrinde, what has happened? You look like you've fought every step of the way here.'

'What you say is not far from the truth. I am Lancearon's ambassador here, an observer more than a contestant. The mysterious tournament seemed like a good opportunity not only to learn what Kulothiel is up to, but also to make contact with our Kalimari kindred. So Astacar, Linvion and I were sent. Yet we had not gotten far beyond the borders of the old empire when we were ambushed. It was a gang of Aranese outlaws. Thieves, rogues and murderers. They are led by a captain named Raspald, whom his followers name Kin-slayer.'

'How many were they?' Curillian struggled to imagine how mere bandits had discomfited the famous Elrinde, Lancearon's 'holy sword'.

This was an elf who had single-handedly cloven his way through orc armies, a swordsman with no equal in all of Astrom.

'Fifteen.' Anger flickered in Elrinde's face at the admission. Anger and embarrassment. Curillian was speechless. Each of Lancearon's chosen three would normally be worth a hundred others in a fight: deadly, skilled, and lightning-fast.

'How did it happen?'

'I had only slain a couple of the scum before one of them got behind Linvion and took her hostage. She is clever, but more of a diplomat than a soldier. To purchase her life, Astacar and myself had to yield and surrender our weapons. Somehow, they had heard of this Tournament. I was forced to guide them here, in return for which they let Linvion live. They deliberately waylaid us when chance brought into their path just what they needed. They didn't let down their guard the whole way here, until they were distracted by that circus out there. Seizing our chance, we took back our weapons and left them. They have no idea how little they will profit from their cunning. Fools! Oron Amular is holy ground. Even if they had not injured the subjects of Lancearon, they would forfeit their lives for daring to tread here. Each one will die. Raspald Kin-slayer, Benek Thunder-Eye, Sampa the Smooth, Vampana the witch-healer, Sceant, Lucask Lightfoot. They have all been marked.'

Curillian recoiled from the force of Elrinde's words, and only then did he notice the other elf standing by. Clad in various hues of blue, grey-eyed and sombre, he was a sea-elf, older than Elrinde, but no less noble. He smiled graciously at Curillian, showing none of the thirst for vengeance harboured by his companion.

'King Curillian, I am Nimarion, Lord of Marinia and representative of the Marintors. I came with here with two others, representatives of Avatar and Firnar.' That made him a very senior figure in the sea-elf realm, scarce a rank or two junior to Marintor himself, the sea-elf king. 'Your reputation is well-merited, for it has been borne out by your conduct here. I see and hear that you have established a truce between all these volatile guests, for which I am grateful, on behalf of all my kindred. It would not do for blood to be spilled before the Tournament has started, but it would have gone particularly ill for those at fault. The Mountain is not as blind as many here might suppose. Kulothiel knows you are here. He is ready for you, and he will summon you soon. Fare thee well, king of the armists.' In one suave motion, Nimarion turned to go, but Curillian checked him.

'Please, lord, before you go. Do you know what this is all about? What is Kulothiel up to?' Nimarion lowered his sad, benevolent eyes to Curillian's, and spoke soothingly.

'The Keeper is his own master. His full devices and true purposes are known to none, not even the wise in Paeyeir. We shall see…but you, Curillian, have as good a chance as anyone here of finding out the truth when all is finished. But survive the many snares before you, or Mariston will never know why her king died.'

A

The elves were gone in a rustle of robes and soft feet. Curillian's heart was heavy, grieving at the thought that his old friendship with Elrinde was forgotten. So many friendships won and lost over the years. For the first time he felt old. Old and tired.

The night passed, and the long-awaited day dawned. Curillian awoke refreshed and revitalized, the lethargy of the previous night fading like a thought. Not all seemed to share his energy. Some were excited, itching for the off, some were scared, and all were nervous. The day was hot and the air humid. A stifling atmosphere lay over the various camps, where elf, man, dwarf and armist kept studied distance between each other. Frugal meals were eaten half-heartedly, and private thoughts were nursed in a thousand internal conversations.

The armists broke open their packs and dressed for action. Their travelling clothes were stowed and exchanged for battle-wear, leather and mail. Routine took over as kit was checked and weapons sharpened. Curillian called them all together as the light was fading.

'My friends, the time is nearly upon us. This is what we've come all the way from Mariston for. There will be danger inside, and great fear. As such, I do not command any of you to enter; but I welcome the company of each one of you who comes willingly. Lancoir, Antaya, Findor, Aleinus, Andil, Lionenn, Caréysin and Roujeark, there are none I'd rather have beside me. Many challenges and tests both stern and strange lie before us, so let us be prepared. Remember, our brains will be needed just as much as our muscles. Do not assume anything in there is safe, so touch cautiously and tread lightly. Look around you. Some here are allies, friends, grudging admirers, and plenty too are enemies from of old. Once we get inside, we're on our own, and we'll need to stick together. Antaya, say a prayer for us.'

The devout guard led them in earnest prayer. On behalf of all of them, he besought Prélan for protection and guidance, wisdom and strength…and success. When he finished, their eyes met, and they all clasped wrists. They were ready.

And they waited.

The whole valley waited. Fuller than it had been for centuries, all eyes were turned towards the Mountain, elves, men, dwarves and armists alike. As darkness fell, no one so much as thought of food or sleep. Warriors fidgeted and fiddled with weapons, and lords stalked back and forth. The darkness deepened, and still nothing happened.

Roujeark, though, felt something that no one else did. He sensed the onset of something in the dark. Eerie winds picked up and rushed tauntingly among them, but behind the unsettling sound, he felt the air prickle. His fingertips tingled, as if responding to some unseen force. The air thickened so much it took his very breath. The Mountain seemed to intensify its magnetism, tugging him towards it. He raised his eyes, and watched the full moon rise above the icy ridges and escarpments. Curillian saw it too, and held his breath. Roujeark's stomach lurched and all around him cringed, as if some invisible irritant stung their ears. From deep within the Mountain, a vast pressure rose up and up until it burst from the summit like a volcano. An eruption of light and sound shook the still night air, illuminating the valley floor like daylight. In the sudden glare, the icy flanks of the Mountain glimmered fell and terrible.

Even as the first eruption subsided, a second explosion of lights went off much lower down the mountainside, kindling an archway of fire above a narrow shelf. All eyes strained up towards that sight, wondering what it heralded. Slowly the fires subsided and went out. They saw that the shelf where the lights had been could be reached by a steep but viable slope up over the Mountain's toes.

In ones and twos, small groups, and wary companies, they were drawn towards it, all under the same spell. If some had thoughts of turning back, none now found it possible. Even those who quailed inwardly realised that their feet were summoned. Fears heightened and bowels clenched, but all kept going forward. They quite forgot each other, heedless of the friends, foes, and soon-to-be-rivals that advanced all around them. The contestants scaled the lowest paths of the Mountain like ants, slowly converging on that shelf where the beacon had burned.

Gradually the path beneath their feet became smoother and broader until it led them up onto the shelf and beneath a tall, smooth cliff-face. As they arrived, they saw a dark outline in the lower portion of the cliff, a great rectangle of glowing runes. The lights and fires had gone out, but the runes still gleamed in the night. They framed a great dark door, but faintly visible in the darkness. The first men to arrive approached it nervously, but soon came up short. The way was shut.

As the armists came up behind, they could hear the mixture of fear, disappointment and consternation rippling through the crowd of questers in front of them.

'It's locked,' some cried.

'There's no way in,' others wailed, their voices stinging the cold night air.

Gradually a passage opened up before them and Curillian and his company found themselves drawn forwards to the front. When they got there, they could see what had been hidden before. The door was indeed shut. It loomed over their heads, dwarfing all of them. It was featureless except for a circular impression halfway between the doorposts. Roujeark's eye was drawn there immediately and he could hear his heart thudding within him. Almost without thinking, his hand went to the star-seal beneath his clothes. His fingers seemed to get a shock as they brushed its cold metal. Roujeark jumped as he felt Curillian's hand laid on his arm. He found the king looking at him, almost as if he had had the same thought. They alone knew that the young armist bore the seal, but now he slowly drew it out.

As he stepped forward, the others around him became aware of him and dropped back. A buzz and a murmur arose as they regarded him, wondering what he was going to do. Roujeark could feel their eyes on his back as he took another step forward, cradling the star-seal uncertainly in his hands. He looked around for the elves, feeling sure that they would know what to do, or even that this was something for them to do. But no sooner had he located their bright eyes in the crowd than they melted into the darkness, ceding to him.

He looked back at the crowd of faces, men stern and women proud, dwarves in their fearsome helms and his own armist companions. He quailed under their expectation, and looked to Curillian for reassurance. The king just nodded. Behind him loomed Sir Theonar, who gestured forwards with his hand. Swallowing hard, Roujeark turned back to the door and approached it with trembling steps. Visions of his former days rushed through his mind, all insisting that his whole life had led him here, to this moment.

The closer he got, the more detail he saw in the circular feature. It was a raised area standing proud of the dark doors, and a circle of glowing light ran around it like a residual fire from the explosion of lights. Inside the circle was a carved surface full of runes. He could not read them, but the star-shaped impression in their midst was unmistakeable. Raising the star-seal, he found that it was the exact same shape. With a trembling hand, he lifted it and slotted it into the indent. It sank neatly into place and did...nothing.

Nothing happened. Roujeark's heart continued thudding but he could almost hear the collectively-held breath behind his back. A few more agonising seconds past, and then the seal began to glow. A word was illuminated amongst the runes. It flashed bright and the seal dropped out of its fitting with a loud, startling hiss. Roujeark stepped back in fear, and the entire crowd behind him went back several paces also, cringing away as if expecting to be struck down. Hesitantly Roujeark leaned down to retrieve the fallen seal, and as he did so, he felt rather than saw the doors swing inwards. They did so soundlessly, and so dark was it inside that only the disappearance of the glowing circle and its fitting persuaded him that the doors really had opened. A waft of suppressed air issued forth and the night air seemed to crackle and fizz, suddenly alive.

The whole host of questers was suddenly under some strange compulsion. The spell allowed for no hesitation, no second thoughts. They entered inside as if drawn by some great pressure within. Elves of Kalimar and Ithrill, dwarves of Carthak, mortals of Hendar, Ciricen, Aranar and Lurallan, they all plunged into the blackness. Roujeark resisted the tug long enough on the threshold to turn his eyes upward and behold the forbidding bulk of the Mountain soaring steep overhead. The moon-washed heights of ice and rock, framed against the pale stars, was the last thing he saw before darkness engulfed him.

Λ

Here ends Rite of Passage, Book II of Oron Amular.
Look out for
Book III: Power Unimaginable, coming soon.

INSIDE The Mountain the darkness was complete. For the first few steps they had been aided by the faint moonlight outside, long enough to see that they were in a tunnel, but very soon they must have turned a corner, for even that small light was lost, plunging them into utter blackness. Roujeark's eyes strained uselessly against the darkness, but he couldn't even see his hand in front of his face. He could hear, though. Hear the sound of others blundering blindly up ahead, of feet scuffling and armour clinking, of curses muttered under various breaths and the nervous calls of one to one another. Yet even those sounds seemed to fade after a while, as if the various parties were being separated and devoured by the terrible darkness, one by one.

Roujeark reached out his hand to feel for the tunnel wall, but it was further away than he thought. Straining for it, he nearly fell over before coming to rest against it. To his surprise, the rock wasn't rough, but smooth to touch. Feeling with fingers and feet, he found that both the wall and the floor were smooth as polished gems and flat as paving slabs. No blemishes or snags could he find. But he had only gone a few doubtful steps when he bumped into something. It was one of his companions. Clutching the arm, Roujeark felt the armist quivering.

'Who is that?' he whispered, hearing his words vanish in the swallowing darkness.

'Aleinus,' came the barely audible reply. In fact, they were all here, stopped dead in the middle of the tunnel. Groping darkness was before them and behind them, above them and below them. The very air was thick with potency, harsh to taste and seeming to tingle on the tongue and fingertips. In the face of this invisible barrier the lion-hearted armists faltered, unnerved and uncertain. Here normal boldness was of no avail. Even Curillian was at a loss. When Roujeark discovered the king by touch, he found him still and tense, confronting the impenetrable darkness. Long moments passed in silence, with only the sound of shallow breathing hanging in the air. Slowly, Roujeark stepped forward. The air seemed to be full of whispering spirits, murmuring long-forgotten secrets and creeds. He was terrified, but the feel of this place, heavy, forbidding, mysterious, was slightly less daunting for him than for his companions. He felt some sort of affinity with it.

He stepped forward into the watchful air, having to drag himself against unseen resistance. Even with so little a step he had moved out of touching distance of his companions, but after a heartbeat or two the king moved up behind him. Curillian was completely out of his comfort-zone, but his courage was conquering his fear. Lancoir defaulted to sticking as close to his king as possible, and each armist followed suit, all afraid of being left behind in the gloom. Roujeark had them link hands and stretch out so they could fill the tunnel, touching it on either side. Yet it was wider than any of them had imagined, a vast corridor fit for princes. The wide space quite belied the sluggish movement of the airs and cheated noises, which seemed not to behave as normal. But stretched out, and hands joined, they felt slightly more at ease, and proceeded cautiously forward.

Reluctantly, the blanket darkness gave way before them. Now and again they felt the tickle of some wind filtering down from an unseen vent above their heads, and occasionally they caught muffled sounds from ahead. With a veritable army ahead of them, they might have expected to hear more, but the sounds just weren't carrying. Nerves tautened like harp-strings and hairs stood on end as each member of the company began imagining what end had already befallen their competitors. Their powers of reason and deduction seemed to have been left behind outside, like their courage, so they found themselves at the mercy of their senses, quite convinced by the distortions that were being reported to them by eyes, ears and noses. The cool night from outside had been replaced by a stuffy heat, such that beads of sweat started to form on their brows and hands, and they twitched and crackled, as if toyed with by delinquent sparks in the air.

They followed the tunnel, feeling it bend and twist in slow, deliberate curves. The darkness seemed to lessen an iota, or so their hopeful eyes claimed, but still nothing definite could they see. Their feet were more certain in reporting a gradient and, following that long smooth slope, they came to a place where the tunnel walls gave out on either side. The air suddenly felt very different. Still queer and laden with intent, it now scurried about and carried sound more easily. They began to hear other groups about them. Suddenly sounds seemed to be all round them, of boots scuffing and scabbards banging, of leather creaking and mail clinking, of heavy breathing and sniffing. The place was teeming with life. Voices began to call to each other, some in fear and some in suspicion. Then an almighty clatter split the air as two metal objects collided. The armists drew close and stuck together in a tight group, but even so they bumped and jostled with unseen neighbours.

Roujeark felt the tension ratcheting up inside him as he groped blindly in the intolerable darkness. He felt enclosed and exposed at the same time. With every passing second, he feared a collision or a sly knife sliding out of the jet-black air. Panic was building up within him, ready to burst out in a shrill scream when, all of a sudden, a silver flame burst into life. Poof! Up above them, it seemed to hover in mid-air. Then another joined it, and another. Poof! Poof! Poof! In the blinking of a suddenly seeing eye, there was a ring of silver fires up above them. In their velveteen light, the inhabitants of the hall might have seen one another, except they were all straining their eyes upward. They caught glimpses of ancient grandeur, carvings, friezes and sculpted vaulting, all dancing in a fire-lit ceiling high above. The fires seemed to burn out of sconces set on some sort of raised gallery.

Just as the contestants were adjusting to take in this vague information, a blinding light filled the roof like sheet lightning. A moment later there came a multi-layered boom like rolling fireworks, then cascades of iridescent sparks were falling among them. Those who had the presence of mind raised their shields to ward off the hazard, but still many eyes were dazzled and not a few burns caused. Yet the sparks had not been without purpose, for their passing had ignited wall-torches all around the place, and now there was enough light to see by. Not enough as could be wished, but enough to fit everything else together. The contestants were now able to take one another in, resuming their uneasy acquaintance after what seemed like an eternity. Together they found themselves in a vast and glamorous cavern, like the anteroom of a strange old palace. It was a perfect circle, flat and smooth and painted in a colour that at one moment seemed terracotta and then mahogany the next. There were portraits and engravings everywhere, depicting strange scenes of wizards and magic.

Above these murals, which were uncannily lifelike, there swept a lip of bronze, crowning and encircling the walls. Beyond that lip there seemed to be a circular walkway, lost out of sight. The only thing marking the head of the chamber was a little indent in the bronze lip, where a small balcony jutted out. So awed by their surroundings were they, that it was some time before the contestants noticed the figure standing there, still as stone. The murmuring amongst the company died down as one by one the contestants became aware of the statue-like person above them. Their eyes were drawn irresistibly towards him, and then were locked, unable to look away. The figure was clad in a dark green robe. His long hair was white and silver was the wispy beard that fell to beneath the rim of the wall. He looked old beyond reckoning, but he stood erect, unbent by whatever years lay upon him. His gaunt face was proud and grim, a study in fascination, yet unknowable. Long clever hands rested on the bronze lip in front of him, and a curious staff leaned beside him. Beneath his unwavering gaze, each and every person in the chamber felt like a child, tiny, and inordinately young. After what felt like an eternity, the words came.

'Hail, contestants from afar, the Keeper of the Mountain welcomes you to the Tournament of Oron Amular.'

The words seemed to emanate out of the rock itself, impregnated by the slow march of all the years this chamber had witnessed. They didn't even see his lips move. Quiet but booming, unguessable but certain, each person heard the words as if from within his own head.

'They who were summoned here by invite are welcome, and their retinues with them; but woe to him or her that cometh here unbidden. Guest and intruder alike, both have passed within the doors, and they are now shut. They shall not reopen until the Tournament has run its course. The signal moon waxes in the night sky above, and she shall have passed away ere this business is done.

'Eight doors there are...' Immediately after he said this, eight portions of the spherical wall, in which no join or crack had before been evident, swung noiselessly inward. '...Eight doors, eight routes beyond, and eight leaders to tread the way. Each way leads into the Tournament, and though the aspect of each may vary, each will lead inexorably to the same destination. Which of you can know what you will find upon the way? But verily, at the end awaits the prize which you all seek...Power Unimaginable...'

The last two words echoed and reverberated around the chamber, rumbling on and on, and as they did so the silver fires went out as suddenly as they had been ignited. The wall-torches too were extinguished, and the timeless speaker vanished. The only light that was left was a faint glow around each of the eight newly revealed doorways. As if by some hidden signal, the eight parties gravitated towards their own entrance. Elves of Ithrill went to one, elves of Kalimar to another; the dwarves of Carthak had their own, as too did the armists of Maristonia; and one each was set apart for the men of Hendar, of Ciricen, of Aranar, and of Lurallan. None of them saw the additional opening prepared for the interlopers, they who had seen no invite and followed no flag. None saw them go, but the screams that marked their expulsion from the chamber, like the hunting cries of vampire-demons, transfixed with horror those that heard them.

That terror was only deepened by the menace of the doorways, the eerie light around them and the complete lack of light in the blackness beyond. What lay without? Would they step into a void and tumble into oblivion, or would other horrors be waiting? Some tried to get out of the chamber, back the way they had come, but to their consternation they could find no trace of the broad sloping passage that had brought them hither. While the others were gripped by panic, Roujeark took it upon himself to lead. He stepped under the glowing arch and then into the blackness beyond. His companions were hesitant to follow him into so dark a place, so a sudden idea came to him. He conjured a small flame in the palm of his hand. Turning, he raised it to his companions, shedding a little light on their fearful faces. It looked for all the world like he was holding a small oil lamp. In its small light, they could all see that what lay beyond was just a tunnel, a tunnel like any other. Now revealed, its terror diminished somewhat.

Roujeark could not keep the flame in his palm indefinitely, but just as it was starting to waver, bringing all the guards' fears back, he came across a long disused torch in a wall brazier. Once the torch was alight and burning brightly, the young conjuror handed it to Findor, who looked glad to receive it. Now they could proceed faster, but trepidation still made them slower than they could have been. Roujeark could sense the growing air of hostility. He guessed that obstacles and hurdles awaited them. For a long time, they followed a descending slope which wound and wound round many bends and twists. As they went, the air grew noticeably warmer.

After what seemed like an age of walking, they came to a small cavern. It was much smaller than the main cavern where Kulothiel had met them, but still a curving open space with a low ceiling. Running around the opposite side of the cavern was a series of doors. They all came to a stop, uncertain what to do next. There were six doors, and no clues as to which way to go. Fear rose and magnified the decision: what if they chose wrongly? A poor choice here could be disastrous, sending them plummeting down into an abyss or into a lair of monsters. The torchlight danced about as Findor trembled noticeably. Steeling themselves, Lancoir and the guards tried each door, and found that every one of them opened. No locks to narrow their choice.

Roujeark looked closely at each door, going slowly from one to the next and feeling his hands over them. All were alike, heavy seasoned oak with brass bindings and locks. Yet on one the varnish of long-vanished days was peeling, the brass was tarnished and the wood was slightly discoloured. There was even a different smell from behind it, even though all that could be seen through any of them within the reach of the torch was a dank passageway. A memory fluttered in Roujeark's mind and a warning came to his heart. In the long past journey when he had met Ardir in the mountain tunnel, he had learnt then that the most attractive-looking option was the wrong one. The way which had looked worse in fact turned out to be right. Like a caged bird suddenly set free, this memory whirred around inside his head and then was gone, and he was left looking at the odd door out, the door that seemed older and in worse repair. Its contrast with the others was not as strong as it had been on that far-off day, but he felt sure the same lesson still applied. He motioned to the others.

'I think it's this way,' he told them.

Curillian looked doubtful. 'What makes you say that?'

Roujeark frowned pensively. 'I cannot be sure, but it reminds me of something I encountered long ago. I feel in my heart that Prélan is leading us through here.' Lancoir looked even more dubious than the king, but he had no better suggestion to make. Curillian looked appealingly around the room, as if they had missed something.

'There is nothing else to guide us. So let Prélan lead us aright.'

The old door was opened. And one by one they plunged through.

Character List

Characters listed in alphabetical order, with a syllabic guide to pronunciation and short description for each entry.

ACIL, SIR (Ah-sill) – Man, Hawk Clan Knight from Aranar

ADHANOR (Ad-an-or) – Man, newly-succeeded King of Hendar

AIIYOSHA (Eye-oh-shah) – Elf, chieftain of the Cuherai, the snow-elves of the Black Mountains

ALEINUS (Ah-lee-nus) – Armist, member of Curillian's Royal Guards

ANDIL (An-dil) – Armist, Royal Guardsman; native to the Phirmar

ANRHUS (An-rous) – Man, Culdon's scout

ANTAYA (An-tie-ah) – Armist, member of Curillian's Royal Guards

ARAMIST (Ara-mist) – Armist, younger brother of Curillian who died young

ARDIR (Ar-deer) – Angelic messenger of Prélan, usually taking elven form

ARVAYA (Ar-vaya) – Elf, late king of Kalimar; great-grandfather of Lithan

ARIMAYA (Ah-rih-my-ah) – Armist, late king of Maristonia; grandfather of Curillian

ASTACAR (As-ta-kar) – Elf of Ithrill, companion of Elrinde

ATHRICK (Ath-rick) – Man of Hendar, squire to Adhanor

AVALAR (A-va-lar) – Elf, late king of Kalimar; grandfather of Lithan

AVAR (Ah-var) – Elf, long-dead prince of the Avatar; a relation of Lithan

AVATAR (Ah-vah-tar) – Eldest elf and first High King of Kalimar

BENEK THUNDER-EYE (Ben-ek) – Man of Aranar, member of Raspald's band

CAIASAN (Kya-san) – Man, scribe and healer of the Pegasus Clan

CAREA (Sah-ree-ah) – Elf, princess of the wood-elves

CARÉYSIN (Car-ay-sin) – Armist, army tracker and expert archer

CARMEN (Car-men) – Armist, queen of Maristonia and wife of Curillian

CELKENORÉ (Kel-ken-or-ray) – Man, former Jeantar of Aranar, of the Unicorn Clan

CUHERL (Soo-hurl) – Elf, father of Aiiyosh

CULDON (Kul-don) – Man, Earl of Centaur, a fiefdom of Ciricen

CURILLIAN (Su-rill-ee-an) – Armist, king of Maristonia and husband of Carmen

CYRON (Ky-ron) – Armist, member of Curillian's Royal Guards

DÁCARIEL (Dah-sah-ree-ell) – Elf, queen of Tol Ankil, niece of Carea and mother of the triplets Sin-Solar, Sin-Tolor & Sin-Serin

DAULASTIR (Daw-luh-stee-ah) – Armist, Lord High Chancellor under King Mirkan. He murdered his master and usurped the throne of the young Curillian, before later being overthrown by the prince when he returned from exile

DEÀREG, SIR (Day-ah-regg) – Man, Falcon Clan Knight from Aranar

DENCARIL (Den-kar-ill) – Man of Hendar, Duke of Nalator and uncle of Adhanor

DUBARNIK (Do-bar-nick) – Armist, conjuror and father of Roujeark

EDRIST (Ed-wrist) – Armist, member of Curillian's Royal Guards

ELRINDE (El-rind) – Elf, a statesman representing King Lancearon of Ithrill

EQUERRIN (Eh-queh-rin) – Man of Hendar, physician to Adhanor

FINDOR (Fin-dor) – Armist, member of Curillian's Royal Guards

GARTHAN (Gar-than) – Man, master-of-arms to Earl Culdon

GERENDAYN (Geh-ren-dane) – Wood-elf, antiquary and gatherer of news

HARDOS, SIR (Har-dos) – Man, Pegasus Clan Knight and close ally of Southilar

HAROTH (Hah-roth) – Armist, member of Curillian's Royal Guards

HORUISTAN (Hor-uh-stan) – Armist, general of the 15th legion

HOTH (Hoth) – Dwarf-lord from the subterranean realm of Carthak

IDUNAR (Ee-doo-nar) – Man, late King of Hendar, father of Adhanor

ILLYIR (Ill-year) – Armist, duke of Welton; cousin to Curillian

IORCAR (Yor-kar) – Dwarf, erstwhile Master-Mage of Oron Amular

KASPAIN (Kas-pain) – Man, household warrior of Earl Culdon

KULOTHIEL (Koo-low-thee-ell) – Man, Head of the League of Wizardry and Keeper of Oron Amular

KURUNDAR (Kuh-run-dar) – Man, sorcerer from Urunmar, brother to Kulothiel

LANCEARON (Larn-sa-ron) – High-elf, king of Ithrill and former Silver Emperor

LANCOIR (Larn-swa) – Armist, Captain of the Royal Guards

LINDAL, SIR (Lin-dal) – Man, Unicorn Clan Knight from Aranar

LINVION (Lin-vee-on) – Elf of Ithrill, companion of Elrinde

LIONENN (Lee-oh-nen) – Armist, army tracker and expert archer

LIOTOR (Leo-tor) – Man, former King of Ciricen, father of Thónarion

LITHAN (Lee-than) – Elf, king of Kalimar

LOSATHEN THE LUCKLESS, SIR (Loss-ah-then) – Man of Aranar, a knight errant

LUCASK LIGHTFOOT (Loo-cas-k) – Man of Aranar, member of Raspald's band

MANRION (Man-ree-on) – Armist, member of Curillian's Royal Guards

MARINTOR (Ma-rin-tor) – Elf, king of the eponymous sea-elf kindred, ancestor of Aiiyosh

NARHEYN (Nar-hayn) – Man, household warrior of Earl Culdon

NIMARION (Nim-ah-ree-on) – Elf of Kalimar

NORSCINDE (Nor-sind) – Armist, member of Curillian's Royal Guards

NURVO (Nur-vo) – Man of Hendar, Bishop of Losantum

ONANDUR (Oh-nan-durh) – Man, Earl of Oloyir in Hendar and Captain of Adhanor's bodyguards

PARTHIR (Par-thear) – Man of Raduthon, a barbarian principality in the south

PERETHOR (Peh-reh-thor) – Elf, resident of Faudunum

PIRON (Peer-on) – Armist, junior officer of the third cohort of The Royal Guards; second-in-command to Surumo

PRÉLAN (Pray-larn) – God, deity of the elves and all believing folk. Prélan is one and the same as the Triune God of Christianity. He reveals Himself differently to the inhabitants of Astrom than He has to us on Earth.

RASPALD THE KIN-SLAYER (Ras-pald) – Man of Aranar, bandit chieftain

REUBUN (Roo-bun) – Man of Hendar, Duke of Lalator and favourite of Adhanor

RHYARD (Ry-ard) – Man, household warrior of Earl Culdon

ROMANTHONY, SIR (Row-man-tho-nee) – Man, Eagle Clan Knight from Aranar

ROTHGER (Roth-guh) – Man, a Hendarian sheriff and path-finder

ROUJEARK (Roo-jark) – Armist, a gifted young magician; son of Dubarnik. The second syllable, 'jeark' is pronounced similarly to the South African forename 'Jacques', with an accented first vowel; not like the flat-vowelled English 'Jack' or 'Jake'.

RUFIN (Roo-fin) – Man, household warrior of Earl Culdon

RUMORIL (Roo-mor-ill) – Man of Hendar, Duke of Malator and uncle of Adhanor

SAMPA THE SMOOTH (Sam-pah) – Man of Aranar, member of Raspald's band

SCEANT (Skee-ant) – Man of Aranar, member of Raspald's band

SIN-SERIN (Sin-seh-rin) – Elf, princess of Tol Ankil

SOUTHILAR (Soo-thi-lar) – Man, Jeantar and lord of Aranar, of the Pegasus Clan

SURUMO (Suh-roo-mo) – Armist, commanding officer of the third cohort of The Royal Guards

THEAMACE (Theam-ace) – Horse, favourite mount of Curillian

THEONAR, SIR (Theo-nar) – Man, Pegasus Clan Knight and rival of Southilar

THERENDIR (Theh-ren-deer) – Elf, king of the wood-elves, father of Carea

THÓNARION (Tho-nah-ree-on) – Man, King of Ciricen and liege-lord of Earl Culdon

UTARION (You-tah-ree-on) – Armist, member of Curillian's Royal Guards

VAMPANA (Vam-par-nah) – Man of Aranar, member of Raspald's band

XAVION (Zay-vee-on) – Man of Hendar, Earl of Koros and favourite of Adhanor

The Races of Astrom

A short guide to introduce the main races of Astrom that we meet in Oron Amular. More information on the people and places of Astrom can be found in the online glossary at **www.worldofastrom.com**

Armists

A hardy mountain race originally from the foothills of the Carthaki Mountains. They awoke at the dawn of the Second Chapter, the second of the Free Peoples, and shortly before the coming of the dwarves. Fostered and taught by the elves, they moved into the lowlands and slowly spread across Maristonia, which in the passing of time became their own kingdom. They are a species apart, sharing some features with their elven and mortal neighbours but being quite unlike them in others. As a rule, they are short and stockily-built, are adaptable and persevere well in difficult tasks. They have a reputation for valour and stubbornness.

Dwarves

Like the armists, the dwarves are children of the mountains and they awoke in the Carthaki Mountains at around the same time as the armists. But whereas the armists were befriended and tutored by the elves, becoming like them in their worldview and habits, the dwarves were long isolated in a remote part of Astrom. They had a different temperament, being more secretive, more industrious, and preferring to live underground in excavated halls and caverns. With time they also built an overground civilisation and dwelt side by side with the elven kingdom of Alanmar. In this time of peace, they sent forth colonists and delved halls in many of the far-flung mountains of Astrom, from which came many different breeds of their race, some noble and some less so. After the ruinous Carthaki Wars they shut themselves underground and forsook the outside world. For long centuries they were not heard from at all, but later they did venture forth to participate in the great events of the world. The dwarves are short, rarely exceeding five feet, but incredibly strong. They are excellent craftsmen and ingenious artisans, working wonders in stone, wood, metal and minerals of all kinds. They are fearless tunnelers, hardy mountaineers and formidable warriors. They do not share the elven view of Prélan but have their own conception of the divine and their own law-codes to govern their affairs.

Elves

The elves are the eldest children of Prélan, exalted and excellent among the Free Peoples. They were the first to awake in Astrom, having come to the world in star-capsules. They were known as Avarian, the People of the Stars, but they called themselves Genesi, the First. There are three main kindreds, the Avatar, the Firnai and the Marintors.

The Avatar are the eldest of all, named after their first king, Avatar. Also known as the High-elves, the Avatar are the most senior of the elven kindreds, and also the most populous and powerful. They are great scholars, warriors and craftsmen, preferring to live in cities or in the open country.

Firnai is the elvish name for the Wood-elves, named after their first king, Firnar. The wood-elves are the most secretive of the three main kindreds of the elves, rarely coming out of their woodland fastnesses to interact with the outside world. They are as varied as the trees they love, some loving oaks, some building high homes in giant beeches and some loving riverside willows and alders. They are wonderful weavers, passionate storytellers and great lovers of animals. Some of them even have the gift of shape-shifting into the forms of beasts. Most Firnai dwell deep within Kalimar, but one colony live in the forest of Tol Ankil, on the borders of Maristonia.

Marintors are Sea-elves, dwelling by the coasts and enamoured of all the sea. Dwelling in caves, grottoes and white-walled havens, they are the mariners, explorers and traders of the elves. Their realm once embraced all the coasts of Astrom, but whilst in latter days they may have relinquished much of it to armists and Mortals, they also have innumerable havens and colonies on the far-flung islands and continents of the planet. The Marintors are great singers and lovers of music, but they are also the most worldly of the elves, and the readiest to have dealings with Mortals.

The Cuherai (Snow-elves), who dwell amid the high snows and ice-fields, and the Irynthai (Deep-elves), whose mansions and workshops are underground, are amongst the many lesser kindreds of the elves, but the rest do not feature in this tale.

Harracks

A mysterious race who inhabit subterranean halls and caverns in the land of Stonad. Lying in the southern Black Mountains, this mountainous domain lies between Kalimar proper and the wood-elven realm of Tol Ankil. The harracks are little known to their neighbours except as a source of trouble and few among either armists or elves know the secrets of their origins. In fact, they are an ancient race of dwarves, descended from an outcast chieftain of Carthak who journeyed north in exile with a few followers. These were ignoble individuals who founded a nation which bore their own traits of harshness, injustice and ferocious insularity. Through long millennia of isolation the harracks degenerated into a fallen race of coarse, unlovely warriors and craftsmen, barely recognisable to their old dwarvish kin but not dis-similar from the Black Dwarves of the Goragath Mountains, another evil scion of old Carthak. The harracks are short, stocky and incredibly tough, strong and with thick skin that is difficult to harm. They are ruthless with outsiders and extremely secretive about their ways. However, they do have redeeming features, being quite capable of great feats of engineering, excavation and construction. They are frightful to look upon, for not only were they unlovely to begin with, but they have also added to their horrifying demeanour by affecting brutal customs like head-binding and eschewing all but the most rustic garments and decorations.

Mortals

The elves are the only immortal race among the Free Peoples, and though the armists and dwarves are also mortal, the name Mortals is reserved for those elves who forfeited their immortality for rebellion against Prélan. Though by the time of Oron Amular they may resemble human beings, they are in fact the descendants of elves who fell from grace. In the second half of the Second Chapter, large swathes of the population of Elvendom fell away from the true faith and embraced manifold heresies and false religions. In a cataclysmic event known as the Great Betrayal, those who forsook Prélan were cursed with mortality, losing their deathlessness and many of the virtues of mind and body that went with it. The faithful elves remained in Kalimar and Ithrill, but the Mortals were to be found across much of the rest of Ciroken, in Aranar, Hendar and Ciricen. In all these countries there arose mortal nations and kingdoms which lived uneasily alongside their immortal neighbours. They were still related by blood, but utterly estranged in mindset and values. Mortals were subject to sickness and deformity, as well as ageing, but they made up for their limited years with a great zest for life that expressed itself in invention, literature, art and zealous politics. As such, their realms were characterised by rapid change and frequent upheavals. Had they refrained from fighting each other and amongst themselves, mortal civilisation might have rivalled that of the elves, in accomplishment, if not in longevity. Opinion is divided among the loremasters of Astrom as to whether mortality was in fact a curse, denying Mortals the long bliss of the elves, or a blessing in disguise, speeding their way back to Prélan.

Follow Michael J Harvey
on social media:

Facebook.com/worldofastrom

Twitter: @worldofastrom

Instagram: @worldofastrom

Website: worldofastrom.com

Find out more on goodreads.com by scanning
the QR code below with your smartphone:

Printed in Great Britain
by Amazon

71451849R00129